Men on the Moon

Volume 37

Sun Tracks

An American Indian Literary Series

SERIES EDITOR

Ofelia Zepeda

EDITORIAL COMMITTEE

Vine Deloria, Jr.

Larry Evers

Joy Harjo

N. Scott Momaday

Emory Sekaquaptewa

Leslie Marmon Silko

Men on the Moon

Collected Short Stories by Simon J. Ortiz

The University of Arizona Press   Tucson

First printing

The University of Arizona Press ·

© 1999 by Simon J. Ortiz

All rights reserved

This book is printed on acid-free, archival-quality paper.

Manufactured in the United States of America

04 03 02 01 00 99   6 5 4 3 2 1

Library of Congress Cataloging-in-Publication Data

Ortiz, Simon J., 1941–

Men on the moon: collected short stories/by Simon J. Ortiz.

p.   cm.   —(Sun tracks; v. 37)

ISBN 0-8165-1929-3 (acid-free paper)

ISBN 0-8165-1930-7 (pbk.: acid-free paper)

1. Indians of North America—New Mexico—Social life and customs—
Fiction.   2. Acoma Indians—Social life and customs—
Fiction.   I. Title.   II. Series.

PS501. S85 vol. 37 PS3565.R77

810.8′0054—dc21   98-58145

[813′.54]   CIP

British Library Cataloguing-in-Publication Data

A catalogue record for this book is available from the British Library.

The stories reproduced here were originally published, some of them in a somewhat different form, in *Fightin': New and Collected Stories, Howbah Indians,* and *The Man to Send Rain Clouds.*

For my beloved children and grandchildren,

and for my beloved people and the land,

who will always be with each other.

Contents

Preface

Story speaks for you. Story speaks for me. Simply put, story speaks for us. There is no other way to say it. That's a basic and primary and essential concept. Story has its own power, and the language of story is of that power. We are within it, and we are empowered by it. We exist because of it. We don't exist without that power. As human beings, we, as personal and social cultural entities, are conscious beings because of story, no other reason.

I've known "story"—or stories—all my life, just like everyone else. For me, there's never been a conscious moment without story. That's simply the case, that's simply fact. Cultural consciousness, whether personal and individual or social and collective, is determined by our awareness of the self within circumstance, experience, and event. Place and time and motion: something happening.

Telling about a place: where you're from, for example, or where you've been. And what happened there. When, how, why. Your consciousness of something going on, of something taking place: that's story. What else could it be?

I don't recall being born. But I do know my life to some degree and in some detail. I don't completely know the explicit details of my Acoma cultural birth (conceptualization and existence; origin and continuance). But I do know the fact of my present reality as a person with an Acoma heritage, and I know the circumstances, experiences, events that I as a personal and social entity have gone through, including many changes.

Therefore, my identity as a Native American is based on the knowledge of myself as a person from Acoma Pueblo, a cultural and geographical place, and this knowledge has its source in "story." To me, identity is dependent upon story. And to Native people whose aboriginal or indigenous identity is precolonial (that is, before white cultural civilization), oral narrative is "story."

Oral tradition narrative was the way in which culture and cultural knowledge was conveyed from the past to the present, from the old days to the modern age, from older to younger generations. And contrary to those who say the "old ways" are dissipating and disappearing, oral tradition narrative is still the main way in which human cultural knowledge is conveyed today.

Although, obviously, written language is very prominent, and unfortunately predominant in some ways, oral language is still the major way we affect each other. I'm a great believer in the intimacy and immediacy of story when it has that quality and orientation of the oral tradition narrative, and this is what I hope the stories in this collection convey.

These are stories from the latter 1960s, and a number from the 1970s and the early 1980s. I've left most of them intact and relatively unchanged except for minor changes and "corrections." Rereading previous writing—just like telling old stories—always involves change, which seems to have to do with how and what we're feeling and thinking presently. And I've rewritten, revised, and changed some stories, although I've kept them in their original form as much as possible.

Working again on the stories or just rereading them is an enjoyable visit for me. I learn something from the visit—perhaps it feels like visiting myself "back then." My enjoyment has been a motivation for this collection since a friend mentioned to me that there is a younger generation of readers and listeners who don't know my early stories—who might learn something from the visit and enjoy the stories.

I am thankful—always and forever truly—to Raho, Rainy, and Sara (all precious ones) for their love and continuing belief in me as father and writer.

Thanks also to the Lila Wallace–Reader's Digest Fund.

Simon J. Ortiz
Tucson, Arizona

Men on the Moon

Men on the Moon

Joselita brought her father, Faustin, the TV on Father's Day. She brought it over after Sunday mass, and she had her son hook up the antenna. She plugged the TV cord into the wall socket.

Faustin sat on a worn couch. He was covered with an old coat. He had worn that coat for twenty years.

It's ready. Turn it on and I'll adjust the antenna, Amarosho told his mother. The TV warmed up and then the screen flickered into dull light. It was snowing. Amarosho tuned it a bit. It snowed less and then a picture formed.

Look, Naishtiya, Joselita said. She touched her father's hand and pointed at the TV.

I'll turn the antenna a bit and you tell me when the picture is clear, Amarosho said. He climbed on the roof again.

After a while the picture turned clearer. It's better! his mother shouted. There was only the tiniest bit of snow falling.

That's about the best it can get, I guess, Amarosho said. Maybe it'll clear up on the other channels. He turned the selector. It was clearer on another channel.

There were two men struggling mightily with each other. Wrestling, Amarosho said.

Do you want to watch wrestling? Two men are fighting, Nana. One of them is Apache Red. Chisheh tsah, he told his grandfather.

The old man stirred. He had been staring intently into the TV. He wondered why there was so much snow at first. Now there were two men fighting. One of them was a Chisheh—an Apache—and the other was a Mericano. There were people shouting excitedly and clapping hands within the TV.

The two men backed away from each other for a moment and then they clenched again. They wheeled mightily and suddenly one threw the other. The old man smiled. He wondered why they were fighting.

Something else showed on the TV screen. A bottle of wine was being poured. The old man liked the pouring sound and he moved his mouth and lips. Someone was selling wine.

The two fighting men came back on the TV. They struggled with each other, and after a while one of them didn't get up. And then another man came and held up the hand of the Apache, who was dancing around in a feathered headdress.

It's over, Amarosho announced. Apache Red won the fight, Nana.

The Chisheh won. Faustin stared at the other fighter, a light-haired man who looked totally exhausted and angry with himself. The old man didn't like the Apache too much. He wanted them to fight again.

After a few minutes, something else appeared on the TV.

What is that? Faustin asked. In the TV picture was an object with smoke coming from it. It was standing upright.

Men are going to the moon, Nana, Amarosho said. That's Apollo. It's going to fly three men to the moon.

That thing is going to fly to the moon?

Yes, Nana, his grandson said.

What is it called again? Faustin asked.

Apollo, a spaceship rocket, Joselita told her father.

The Apollo spaceship stood on the ground, emitting clouds of something, something that looked like smoke.

A man was talking, telling about the plans for the flight, what would happen, that it was almost time. Faustin could not understand the man very well because he didn't know many words in the language of the Mericano.

He must be talking about that thing flying in the air? he said.

Yes. It's about ready to fly away to the moon.

Faustin remembered that the evening before he had looked at the sky and seen that the moon was almost in the middle phase. He wondered if it was important that the men get to the moon.

Are those men looking for something on the moon, Nana? he asked his grandson.

They're trying to find out what's on the moon, Nana. What kind of dirt and rocks there are and to see if there's any water. Scientist men don't believe there is any life on the moon. The men are looking for knowledge, Amarosho said to Faustin.

Faustin wondered if the men had run out of places to look for knowledge on the earth. Do they know if they'll find knowledge? he asked.

They have some already. They've gone before and come back. They're going again.

Did they bring any back?

They brought back some rocks, Amarosho said.

Rocks. Faustin laughed quietly. The American scientist men went to search for knowledge on the moon and they brought back rocks. He kind of thought that perhaps Amarosho was joking with him. His grandson had gone to Indian School for a number of years, and sometimes he would tell his grandfather some strange and funny things.

The old man was suspicious. Sometimes they joked around. Rocks. You sure that's all they brought back? he said. Rocks!

That's right, Nana, only rocks and some dirt and pictures they made of what it looks like on the moon.

The TV picture was filled with the rocket spaceship close-up now. Men were sitting and standing and moving around some machinery, and the TV voice had become more urgent. The old man watched the activity in the picture intently but with a slight smile on his face.

Suddenly it became very quiet, and the TV voice was firm and commanding and curiously pleading. Ten, nine, eight, seven, six, five, four, three, two, one, liftoff. The white smoke became furious, and a muted rumble shook through the TV. The rocket was trembling and the voice was trembling.

It was really happening, the old man marveled. Somewhere inside of that cylinder with a point at its top and long slender wings were three men who were flying to the moon.

The rocket rose from the ground. There were enormous clouds of smoke and the picture shook. Even the old man became tense, and he grasped the edge of the couch. The rocket spaceship rose and rose.

There's fire coming out of the rocket, Amarosho explained. That's what makes it fly.

Fire. Faustin had wondered what made it fly. He had seen pictures of other flying machines. They had long wings, and someone had explained to him that there was machinery inside which spun metal blades that made the machines fly. He had wondered what made this thing fly. He hoped his grandson wasn't joking him.

After a while there was nothing but the sky. The rocket Apollo had disappeared. It hadn't taken very long, and the voice on the TV wasn't excited anymore. In fact, the voice was very calm and almost bored.

I have to go now, Naishtiya, Joselita told her father. I have things to do.

Me too, Amarosho said.

Wait, the old man said, wait. What shall I do with this thing? What is it you call it?

TV, his daughter said. You watch it. You turn it on and you watch it.

I mean how do you stop it? Does it stop like the radio, like the mahkina? It stops?

This way, Nana, Amarosho said and showed his grandfather. He turned a round knob on the TV and the picture went away.

He turned the knob again, and the pictured flickered on again. Were you afraid this one-eye would be looking at you all the time? Amarosho laughed and gently patted the old man's shoulder.

Faustin was relieved. Joselita and her son left. Faustin watched the TV picture for a while. A lot of activity was going on, a lot of men were moving among machinery, and a couple of men were talking. And then the spaceship rocket was shown again.

The old man watched it rise and fly away again. It disappeared again. There was nothing but the sky. He turned the knob and the picture died away. He turned it on and the picture came on again. He turned it off. He went outside and to a fence a short distance from his home. When he finished peeing, he zipped up his pants and studied the sky for a while.

II

That night, he dreamed.

Flintwing Boy was watching a Skquuyuh mahkina come down a hill. The mahkina made a humming noise. It was walking. It shone in the sunlight. Flintwing Boy moved to a better position to see. The mahkina kept on moving toward him.

The Skquuyuh mahkina drew closer. Its metal legs stepped upon trees and crushed growing flowers and grass. A deer bounded away frightened. Tsushki came running to Flintwing Boy.

Anahweh, Tsushki cried, trying to catch his breath.

What is it, Anahweh? You've been running, Flintwing Boy said.

The coyote was staring at the thing, which was coming toward them. There was wild fear in his eyes.

What is that, Anahweh? What is that thing? Tsushki gasped.

It looks like a mahkina, but I've never seen one quite like it before. It must be some kind of Skquuyuh mahkina, Anahweh, Flintwing Boy said. When he saw that Tsushki was trembling with fear, he said, Sit down, Anahweh. Rest yourself. We'll find out soon enough.

The Skquuyuh mahkina was undeterred. It walked over and through everything. It splashed through a stream of clear water. The water boiled and streaks of oil flowed downstream. It split a juniper tree in half with a terrible crash. It crushed a boulder into dust with a sound of heavy metal. Nothing stopped the Skquuyuh mahkina. It hummed.

Anahweh, Tsushki cried, what can we do?

Flintwing Boy reached into the bag hanging at his side. He took out an object. It was a flint arrowhead. He took out some cornfood.

Come over here, Anahweh. Come over here. Be calm, he motioned to the frightened coyote. He touched the coyote in several places on his body with the arrowhead and put cornfood in the palm of his hand.

This way, Flintwing Boy said. He closed Tsushki's fingers over the cornfood. They stood facing east. Flintwing Boy said, We humble ourselves again. We look in your direction for guidance. We ask for your protection. We humble our poor bodies and spirits because only you are the power and the source and the knowledge. Help us, then. That is all we ask.

Flintwing Boy and Tsushki breathed on the cornfood, then took in the breath of all the directions and gave the cornfood unto the ground.

Now the ground trembled with the awesome power of the Skquuyuh mahkina. Its humming vibrated against everything.

Flintwing Boy reached over his shoulder and took several arrows from his quiver. He inspected them carefully and without any rush he fit one to his bowstring.

And now, Anahweh, Flintwing Boy said, you must go and tell everyone. Describe what you have seen. The people must talk among themselves and learn what this is about, and decide what they will do. You must hurry, but you must not alarm the people. Tell them I am here to meet the Skquuyuh mahkina. Later I will give them my report.

Tsushki turned and began to run. He stopped several yards away. Hahtrudzaimeh! he called to Flintwing Boy. Like a man of courage, Anahweh, like our people.

The old man stirred in his sleep. A dog was barking. He awoke fully and got out of his bed and went outside. The moon was past the midpoint, and it would be daylight in a few hours.

III

Later, the spaceship reached the moon.

Amarosho was with his grandfather Faustin. They watched a TV replay of two men walking on the moon.

So that's the men on the moon, Faustin said.

Yes, Nana, there they are, Amarosho said.

There were two men inside of heavy clothing, and they carried heavy-looking equipment on their backs.

The TV picture showed a closeup of one of them and indeed there was a man's face inside of glass. The face moved its mouth and smiled and spoke, but the voice seemed to be separate from the face.

It must be cold, Faustin said. They have on heavy clothing.

It's supposed to be very cold and very hot on the moon. They wear special clothes and other things for protection from the cold and heat, Amarosho said.

The men on the moon were moving slowly. One of them skipped like a boy, and he floated alongside the other.

The old man wondered if they were underwater. They seem to be able to float, he said.

The information I have heard is that a man weighs less on the moon than he does on earth, Amarosho said to his grandfather. Much less, and he floats. And there is no air on the moon for them to breathe, so those boxes on their backs carry air for them to breathe.

A man weighs less on the moon, the old man thought. And there is no air on the moon except for the boxes on their backs. He looked at Amarosho, but his grandson did not seem to be joking with him.

The land on the moon looked very dry. It looked like it had not rained for a long, long time. There were no trees, no plants, no grass. Nothing but dirt and rocks, a desert.

Amarosho had told him that men on earth—scientists—believed there was no life on the moon. Yet those men were trying to find knowledge on the moon. Faustin wondered if perhaps they had special tools with which they could find knowledge even if they believed there was no life on the moon.

The mahkina sat on the desert. It didn't make a sound. Its metal feet were planted flat on the ground. It looked somewhat awkward. Faustin searched around the mahkina, but there didn't seem to be anything except the dry land on the TV. He couldn't figure out the mahkina. He wasn't sure whether it moved and could cause harm. He didn't want to ask his grandson that question.

After a while, one of the bulky men was digging in the ground. He carried a long, thin tool with which he scooped up dirt and put it into a container. He did this for a while.

Is he going to bring the dirt back to earth too? Faustin asked.

I think he is, Nana, Amarosho said. Maybe he'll get some rocks too. Watch.

Indeed, several minutes later, the man lumbered over to a pile of rocks and gathered several handsized ones. He held them out proudly. They looked just like rocks from around anyplace. The voice on the TV seemed to be excited about the rocks.

They will study the rocks, too, for knowledge?

Yes, Nana.

What will they use the knowledge for, Nana?

They say they will use it to better mankind, Nana. I've heard that. And to learn more about the universe in which we live. Also, some of the scientists say the knowledge will be useful in finding out where everything began a long time ago and how everything was made in the beginning.

Faustin looked with a smile at his grandson. He said, You are telling me the true facts, aren't you?

Why, yes, Nana. That's what they say. I'm not just making it up, Amarosho said.

Well then, do they say why they need to know where and how everything began? Hasn't anyone ever told them?

I think other people have tried to tell them but they want to find out for themselves, and also they claim they don't know enough and need to know more and for certain, Amarosho said.

The man in the bulky suit had a small pickax in his hand. He was striking at a boulder. The breathing of the man could be heard clearly. He seemed to be working very hard and was very tired.

Faustin had once watched a work crew of Mericano drilling for water. They had brought a tall mahkina with a loud motor. The mahkina would raise a limb at its center to its very top and then drop it with a heavy and loud metal clang. The mahkina and its men sat at one spot for several days, and finally they found water.

The water had bubbled out weakly, gray-looking, and did not look drinkable at all. And then the Mericano workmen lowered the mahkina, put their equipment away, and drove away. The water stopped flowing. After a couple of days, Faustin went and checked out the place.

There was nothing there except a pile of gray dirt and an indentation in the ground. The ground was already dry, and there were dark spots of oil-soaked dirt.

Faustin decided to tell Amarosho about the dream he had had.

After the old man finished, Amarosho said, Old man, you're telling me the truth now, aren't you? You know that you've become somewhat of a liar. He was teasing his grandfather.

Yes, Nana. I have told you the truth as it occurred to me that night. Everything happened like that except I might not have recalled everything about it.

That's some story, Nana, but it's a dream.

It's a dream, but it's the truth, Faustin said.

I believe you, Nana, his grandson said.

IV

Sometime after that the spacemen returned to earth. Amarosho told his grandfather they had splashed down in the ocean.

Are they alright? Faustin asked.

Yes, Amarosho said. They have devices to keep them safe.

Are they in their homes now?

No, I think they have to be someplace where they can't contaminate anything. If they brought back something from the moon that they weren't supposed to, they won't pass it on to someone else, Amarosho said to his grandfather.

What would that something be?

Something harmful, Nana.

In that dry desert land of the moon there might be something harmful, the old man said. I didn't see any strange insects or trees or even cactus. What would that harmful thing be, Nana?

Disease which might harm people on earth, Amarosho said.

You said there was the belief by the men that there is no life on the moon. Is there life after all? Faustin asked.

There might be the tiniest bit of life.

Yes, I see now, Nana. If the men find even the tiniest bit of life on the moon, then they will believe, the old man said.

Yes. Something like that.

Faustin figured it out now. The Mericano men had taken that trip in a spaceship rocket to the moon to find even the tiniest bit of life. And when they found even the tiniest bit of life, even if it was harmful, they would believe that they had found knowledge. Yes, that must be the way it was.

He remembered his dream clearly now. The old man was relieved.

When are those two men fighting again, Nana? he asked Amarosho.

What two men?

Those two men who were fighting with each other the day those Mericano spaceship men were flying to the moon.

Oh, those men. I don't know, Nana. Maybe next Sunday. You like them?

Yes. I think the next time I will be cheering for the Chisheh. He'll win again. He'll beat the Mericano again, Faustin said.

Home Country

Well, it's been a while. I think in 1947 was when I left. My husband was killed in Okinawa some years before. And so I had no more husband. And I had to make a living. Oh I guess I could have looked for another man, but I didn't want to. It looked like the war had made some of them into a bad way, anyway. I saw some of them come home like that. They either got drunk or just stayed around for a while or couldn't seem to be satisfied anymore with what was there. At home. I guess, now that I think about it, that happened to me too, although I wasn't in the war, not in the army, or even much off the reservation, just that several years at the Indian School. Well, there was that feeling things were changing, not only the men, the boys, but other things were changing too.

One day, the home nurse that came from the Indian Health Service was at my mother's hogan—my mother was getting near the end real sick—and she said that she had been meaning to ask me a question. I said, What is the question? And the home nurse said, Well, your mother is getting real sick and after she is no longer around for you to take care of, what will you be doing? You and her are the only ones here. And I said, I don't know. But I was thinking about it. What she said made me think about it more. And then the next time she came, she said to me, Eloise, the government is hiring Indians now in the Indian Schools to take care of the boys and girls. I heard one of the supervisors say that Indians are hard workers, but you have to supervise them a lot. And I thought of you, well, because you've been taking care of your mother real good and you follow all my instructions. She said, I thought of you because you're a good Indian girl and you would be the kind of person for that job. I didn't say anything. I had not ever really thought of a job, but I kept thinking about it.

Well, my mother, she died. We buried her up at the old place, the cemetery there. It's real nice on the east side of the hill where the sun shines warm and the wind doesn't blow too much sand around right there. Well, I was sad. We were all sad for a while, but you know how things are. One of my aunties came over, and she advised me and warned me about being too sad about it and all that. She wished me that I would not worry too much about it because old folks they go along pretty soon. Life is that way. And then she said maybe I ought to take in one of my other aunties' kids or two, because there was a lot of them kids and I was all by myself now. I was so young, and I thought I might do that—you know, take care of someone. But I had been thinking, too, of what the home nurse said to me about working. Hardly anybody at home was working at something like that—no woman anyway. And I would have to move away.

Well, I did just that. I remember that day very well. I told my aunties, and they were all crying, and we all went up to the old highway where the bus to town passed by every day. I was wearing an old kind of bluish sweater that was kind of big, that one of my cousins who was older had gotten from a white person, a tourist, one summer in trade for something my cousin had made, a real pretty basket. She gave me that, and I used to have a picture of me with it on. It's kind of real ugly. Yes, that was the day I left, wearing a baggy sweater and carrying a suitcase that someone gave me too, I think, or maybe it was the home nurse. There wasn't much in it anyway. I was scared, and everybody seemed to be sad. I was so young and skinny then. My auntie said, one of them who was real fat, you make sure you eat now. Make your own tortillas, drink the milk, stuff like candies is no good. She learned that from the nurse. Make sure you got your letter, my other auntie said. I had it folded into my purse. Yes, I had one too, a brown one that my husband when he was alive he brought it on my birthday one time on furlough. It was a nice purse and still looked new because I never used it.

The letter said I had a job at Keams Canyon, the Indian Boarding School there, but I would have to go to the Agency first for some papers to be filled out. And that's where I was going first, the Agency. And then they would send me to Keams Canyon, I didn't even know where it was except someone of our relatives said that it was near Hopi. My uncles teased me, saying, Watch out for the Hopi men and boys. Don't let them get too close, they said. Well, you know how they are. They were pretty strict too about those things. They were joking and then they were not joking too, and so I said, Aw, they won't get near to me, I'm too ugly. I promised I would be careful anyway.

So we all gathered for a while at my last auntie's house, and then the old man, Hostiin, my grandfather, brought his wagon and horses to the door. And then we all got in the wagon and sat there for a while until my auntie told her father, Okay, Father, let's go. And shook his elbow because the poor old man was very old by then and kind of going to sleep all the time. You had to talk to him real loud. I had about ten dollars, I think, that was a lot of money—more than it is now, you know. When we got to the highway where the Indian road, which is just a dirt road, goes away from the paved road, my grandfather reached into his blue jeans and pulled out a silver dollar and put it into my hand. I was so shocked. We were all so shocked. We all looked around at each other. We didn't know where the old man had gotten it because we were real poor. Two of my uncles had to borrow on their accounts at the trading store for the money I had in my purse. But there it was, a silver dollar, so big and shiny in my grandfather Hostiin's hand and then in my hand.

Well, I was so shocked, and everybody was so shocked. We all started crying right there at the junction of that Indian road and the paved bilaagahna highway. I wanted to be a little girl again, running after the old man when he hurried with his long legs to the cornfields or went for water down to the river. He was old then, and his eye was turned gray, and he didn't do much anymore except drive his wagon and chop a little bit of wood. But I just held him and I just held him so tightly.

Later on, I don't know what happened to the silver dollar. It had a date of 1907 on it. I kept it for a long time, because I wanted to have it to remember when I left my home country. What I did in between then and now is another story, but that's the time I left my home country.

Howbah Indians

One night I jumped out of bed suddenly.
"Howbah Indians," I said.
"What?" my wife asked.
"I just remembered." I felt good for remembering,
and I wrote it down on a notepad.
Howbah Indians.

"What were you doing?" she asked later.
"I was remembering Eagle," I said.
And then I explained.
"It means you all Indians,
like you Oklahoma folks say: y'all."

Eagle bought a Whiting Brothers gas station, a franchise, up at San Fidel. He used to just work there, wear a khaki uniform with "Whiting Bros" stitched across the right front pocket, and then one day he became the owner of the franchise. He'd be all smiles when he'd come hurrying out of the gas station to fill your car up with two dollars' worth, check your oil, and clean your windshield.

The first thing Eagle did was put up a sign that looked like a couple hundred yards long, you know, like it was a high board fence. The Whiting Brothers gas station chain's colors were yellow and red, and that's what the sign was. Big bright red letters on a bright yellow background.

You could read it ten miles away:

WELCOME HOWBAH INDIANS

It made us proud of Eagle.

I mean, I guess he owned the gas station, or maybe he was only the manager of it, or maybe he only worked there. I'm sure there was some sort of whiteman trader deal involved with it. But that wasn't important. What was important was that the people believed Eagle owned it. And they would joke with him. "Gaimuu shtuumu, nuuyuh kudrah gas station. You don't have to buy gas from Chevron or Conoco or anyone else."

I remember that time Eagle went to Korea. This was back in 1951. He had just gotten out of high school, and I was in the third grade. It was evening when my parents and I walked him up to the highway, which was old US 66 then. It's Interstate 40 now. When we got to the highway, Eagle picked up some gravel stones from the side of the highway and skipped them sideways on the asphalt, and when they'd hit, sparks would fly up. I tried it, and several times sparks flew off the highway for me. The stones must have had flint in them. I can remember all the way from that summer night.

I don't know how long Eagle owned or ran that gas station at San Fidel, but it probably wasn't for very long. The Black Bull Bar was right across the street, right near that bridge that guys from the reservation used to sit under and drink.

Coming to San Fidel from the west, topping the hill, past the Antelope Trading Store, you could see it. I mean it was practically the whole horizon in the east:

WELCOME HOWBAH INDIANS

My father still talks and laughs about one time when he and another man were building a house for old man Pasquale at the village. Eagle was a boy then, and he was mixing mud for them. The other man kept calling Eagle "Payatyamo," teasing him, and the man laughing. When my father and Eagle were walking home in the evening, Eagle asked, kind of worriedly, what "Payatyamo" meant.

My father laughed good-naturedly, and he said to Eagle, "*That's* what it means!" He pointed with his finger to Eagle's crotch! Payatyamo is the name of one of the warrior Kahtzina who has a considerable reputation for his virile manhood!

After Eagle got on the bus and left for training with the Marines in San Diego, I remember the uncertain and gradual welling of sadness in my stomach. My parents and I watched the red taillights of the Greyhound bus as it went westward and disappeared around the bend by Owls Cove. Later on, when it was winter, I worried a lot over the photographs in *Life* magazine that showed Ethiopian soldiers frozen into the snowy ground in Korea.

Well, later on, when Eagle came home and before he bought the gas station, he used to say, "I walked up and down Korea three times. Once, I think, all the way to China, across the Yalu River. Sometimes I can still hear the Chinese, scary at night, their voices yelling down the hills, up the hills."

For a year in the late 1950s, Eagle was appointed Sheriff by the caciques—to get him calmed down from his wild side, the people said, to give him a sense of responsibility.

And then he bought that gas station and put up the sign!

WELCOME HOWBAH INDIANS

A couple of years later—in the early '60s by then, when I was in the U.S. Army, I think—he got lost for a week or so. No one was overly concerned right away, because of the moods Eagle would get into from time to time. The people knew that the moods and the feelings of their young men would sometimes overcome them. They thought maybe Eagle was hanging around Gallup streets or Albuquerque for a few days or maybe even in jail.

But then someone found him in a dry rainwash not far from where he lived with his wife and children. Eagle was lying up against a hard clay bank. He had what looked like bruises from falling on his face or blows with a stone. But the government police from the Bureau of Indian Affairs never bothered about it very much. They never did investigate what happened.

It was winter that time.

So when the guys talk about Eagle now, they say his name in Indian. "Dyaamih." They always spread their arms and hands full out, describing and seeing that bright red and yellow sign on the horizon!

WELCOME HOWBAH INDIANS

They laugh and laugh for the important memory and fact that it is!

Kaiser and the War

Kaiser got out of the state pen when I was in the fourth grade. I don't know why people called him Kaiser. Some called him Hitler too, since he was Kaiser, but I don't think he cared at all what they called him. He was probably just glad to get out of the state pen.

Kaiser got into the state pen because he didn't go into the army. That's what my father said anyway, and according to some people, because he was a nut, which was why he didn't go into the army in the first place, which was what my father said also.

The army wanted him anyway. Or maybe they didn't know he was crazy or supposed to be. They came for him out at home on the reservation, and he said he wasn't going to go because he didn't speak good English. Kaiser didn't go to school more than just the first or second grade. He said what he said in Indian and his sister said it in English for him. The army men, somebody from the county draft board, said they'd teach him English in the army, don't worry about it, and how to read and write. And give him clothes and money when he got out of the army so that he could be regular as any American. Just like anybody else. And they threw in stuff about how it would be good for our tribe and the people of the USA.

Well, Kaiser, who didn't understand that much English anyway, listened quietly to his sister telling him what the army draft board men were saying. He didn't ask any questions, just once in a while said yes like he'd been taught to say in the first grade. Maybe some of the interpretation was lost the way his sister was doing it, or maybe he went nuts like some people said he did once in a while, because the next thing he did was bust out the door and start running for Black Mesa.

The draft board men didn't say anything at first, and then they got pretty mad. Kaiser's sister cried because she didn't want Kaiser to go into the army, but she didn't want him running out just like that either. She had gone to the Indian School in Albuquerque, and she had learned that stuff about patriotism, duty, honor even if you were said to be crazy.

At about that time, grandfather Faustin cussed in Indian at the draft board men. Nobody had noticed when he came into the house, but there he was. Fierce-looking as hell as usual, although he wasn't fierce at all. Then he got mad at his granddaughter and the men, asking what they were doing in his house, making the women cry, and not even sitting down like friendly people did. Old Faustin and the army confronted each other. Needless to say, the army draft board men got pretty nervous. The old man told the girl to go out of the room. He'd talk to the army by himself, although he didn't speak a word of English except "goddammey," which didn't sound too much like English, but he threw it in once in a while anyway.

The army draft board men tried to get the girl to come back into the room, but the old man wouldn't let her. He told her to get to grinding corn or something useful. They tried sign language. When Faustin figured out what they were waving their arms and hands around for, he laughed out loud. He wouldn't even take the cigarettes offered to him, so the army draft board men didn't say anything more. The last thing they did, though, was give old man

Faustin a piece of paper with writing on it. They didn't explain what it was for, but they probably hoped it would get read somehow.

Well, after they left, the paper did get read by the granddaughter. She told Faustin what it was about. The law was going to come and take Kaiser to jail because he wouldn't go into the army by himself. Grandfather Faustin sat still for a while and talked quietly to himself, and then he got up to look for Kaiser.

Kaiser was on his way home by then, and his grandfather told him what was going to happen. They sat down by the side of the road and started to make plans. Kaiser would go hide up on Black Mesa and maybe go all the way to Brushy Mountain if the law really came to poking around seriously. Faustin would take him food and tell him the news once in a while.

Everybody in the village knew what was going on pretty soon. Some people approved of Kaiser hiding on Black Mesa, and some didn't. Some thought it was pretty funny. My father, who couldn't go into the army even if he wanted to because there were too many of us kids, laughed about it for days. The people who approved and thought it funny were the ones who knew Kaiser was crazy. They also said the army must be even crazier. The ones who disapproved were mostly those who were scared of Kaiser. A lot of them were the parents or brothers of girls who they suspected of liking Kaiser.

Kaiser was pretty good-looking and funny in the way he talked for a crazy guy. And he was a hard worker in the cornfields every day or at sheep camp for his parents while they were alive, and very helpful to his sister and nephew and grandfather when they needed help. Those people who were scared of Kaiser and said he should go into the army, perhaps it'll do him good, didn't want him messing around with their daughters and sisters, which they said he would do from time to time. Mostly those people were scared Kaiser would do something. There were too many nuts running around in the village, they said.

My old man didn't care, though. He was buddies with Kaiser. Whenever there was a corn dance at the community hall, they would have a lot of fun singing and laughing and joking. Once in a while when someone brought around a bottle or two, they would really get going, and the officers of the tribe would have to warn them to behave themselves.

Kaiser was okay, though. He came around home quite a lot. His own kinfolks didn't care for him much. They didn't go out of their way to invite him to eat or spend the night when he dropped by their homes and it happened to get dark. My mother didn't mind him around. At meals when she served him something to eat, she didn't act like he was nuts or supposed to be. She just served him and fussed over him like he was a kid, which Kaiser acted like a lot of the time. I guess she didn't figure a guy who acted like a kid was crazy.

Right after we finished eating, if it happened to be supper, my grandfather who was a healer and kiva elder would talk to Kaiser. And to all of us kids really. My grandpa would give us advice and tell us about how the world was and how each person and everything was important. And then he would tell us stories about the olden times, which was always the best part. Legends mostly about the Kahtzina, Spider Old Woman, where our Hanoh came from, how life was in the old days. Some of the stories were pretty funny, some kind of sad, and some kind of boring. Kaiser would sit very still, not saying anything except "Eheh," which is what you're to say once in a while to show that you're listening to the olden times.

After half of us kids were asleep, my grandfather would stop talking, but Kaiser wouldn't want him to stop and he'd ask for more stories. But my grandfather wouldn't tell any more. Then what Kaiser would do was start telling himself about the olden times. He'd lie on the floor in the dark or sometimes on the roof, which was where he'd sleep in the summertime. Talking. Sometimes he would sing, which is also part of the olden times. I would drift off to sleep listening to Kaiser quietly singing and telling stories.

Well, after Kaiser went up on Black Mesa, he didn't come around home. He just went up there and stayed there. The law, which was the County Sheriff and another police officer and the Indian Agent from the Bureau of Indian Affairs office, came out to get him, but nobody would say where he was. The law had a general idea where Kaiser was, but that didn't get them very far because they didn't know the country around Black Mesa. It's rougher than hell up there, just a couple of sheep camps in a lot of country.

The Indian Agent had written a letter to the officials of the tribe saying that the law would come for Kaiser on a certain day. There were a lot of people waiting for the law when they—the Indian Agent, Sheriff, and another policeman—drove up to the community meeting hall. The County Sheriff had a bulging belly, and he had a big six-shooter strapped to his hip. When the men standing outside the meeting hall saw him step out of the government car, they made jokes. "Just like the Long Ranger," someone said. The law didn't know what the Indians were laughing about. They just said hello and didn't pay attention to what they didn't understand.

Grandfather Faustin was among the men. He was silent as he smoked a roll-your-own. The Indian Agent stopped in front of him, and Faustin took a slow drag on his roll-your-own. But he didn't look at the Indian Agent.

"Faustin, my old friend, how are you?" the Indian Agent said.

The old man didn't say anything. He let the tobacco smoke slowly come out of his mouth and nose, and he looked straight ahead. Someone in the crowd told Faustin what the Indian Agent had said, but the old man didn't say anything at all.

Maybe the Indian Agent thought the old man was praying or that he was a wise man contemplating his reply, the way he was so solemn, so he didn't press him. What Faustin was doing was ignoring the law. He didn't want to talk with the law.

He turned to a man at his side. "Tell this man I do not want to talk. I can't understand what they're saying in Mericano anyway. And I don't want anyone to tell me what they say. I'm not interested." Then old Faustin looked at the Indian Agent, the County Sheriff, and the other police officer, and he dismissed their presence with his indignation.

"The old man isn't gonna talk to you," one of the Indians said.

The Indian Agent and Sheriff Big Belly glared at the man who'd spoken. "Who's in charge around here?" the Sheriff demanded loudly.

The Indians laughed. They joked by calling each other Big Belly. The Governor and two Chiefs of the tribe soon came along. They greeted the law, and then they all went into the meeting hall to confer about Kaiser.

"Have you brought Kaiser?" the Indian Agent asked, although he saw they hadn't and knew they wouldn't.

"No," the Governor said. Someone translated it as "He will not come."

"Well, why don't you bring him in? If he doesn't want to come, why don't you bring him in? A bunch of you can bring him," the Indian Agent said. He was getting irritated.

The Governor, Chiefs, and men talked. One elderly man held

the floor a long while until the others grew tired of him telling about the old days, how it was back then, and how the Americans said one thing and did another, and so forth. And then someone said, "We can bring him. Kaiser should come by himself anyway. Let's go get him." This was a man who didn't like Kaiser, and when he finished speaking he looked around him very carefully before sitting down.

"Tell the Mericano that is not the way," one of the Chiefs said. "If our son wants to meet these men, he will come and do so himself."

"I'll be a son of a bitch," the County Sheriff said. When the Indians laughed, the Sheriff glared at them and they stopped. "Let's go get him ourselves," he said angrily.

The man who had been translating from Indian to English said, "He is crazy."

"Who's crazy?" the Sheriff demanded loudly, as if he were refuting an accusation.

"Kaiser, he is crazy," the translator said in a small voice. And he stepped back, somewhat embarrassed.

Grandfather Faustin then came forward. Although he had said he didn't want to talk to them, he shouted at the Indian Agent and the Sheriff, "Go get Kaiser yourself! If he is crazy, I hope he kills you! Go get him!"

"Okay," the Indian Agent said when the translator finished translating what the old man had said. "We'll go get him ourselves. Where is he?" The Indian Agent knew no one would tell him, but he asked anyway.

With that, the Indians assumed that the business the law had come to do was over. The law had resolved what it came to do in the first place. The Indians began to leave.

"Wait! Wait!" the Indian Agent said. "We need someone to go

with us. Kaiser is up on Black Mesa," he said. "But we need some-one to show us where to go." There was some urgency in his voice.

Ignoring the Indian Agent, the Indians kept on leaving the meeting hall. "Halt!" the Indian Agent ordered, but the Indians didn't halt.

"We'll pay you. The government will pay you to go with us," he said, some desperation in his voice. Finally, getting no response, the Indian Agent shouted, "Sheriff, stop them!"

"Stop!" the County Sheriff yelled loudly. "Come back here!" he said, putting a hand on the six-shooter strapped to his bulging waistline.

When they heard the County Sheriff, some of the Indians looked at him to laugh since he sure looked funny and talked funny, but some of them stopped. "All right, you're deputized," the County Sheriff said. And then after taking a look at their faces, he quickly added, "You'll get paid."

Although some of the Indians weren't so sure about getting paid, now the law had some deputies. The law and the Indians piled into the Indian Agent's government car and a pickup truck belonging to one of the deputies, who was told he'd get paid more than the others for the use of his truck.

Black Mesa is fifteen miles back on the reservation. There are only dirt roads, and they aren't very good. Nobody uses them except sheepherders, wood haulers, and deer hunters in the fall. Kaiser knew what he was doing when he went to Black Mesa, and he probably saw them when they approached the mesa. It wouldn't have made any difference because when the law and deputies came to the foot of the mesa they still weren't getting anywhere.

The deputies, who were still Indians, wouldn't tell or didn't really know where Kaiser was at the moment. They all sat for a couple of hours at the foot of the mesa discussing what should be done and where to look. The law tried to get the deputies to talk. The County Sheriff was boiling mad by then, getting madder too, and he was all for "persuading" one of the deputies to tell where Kaiser was exactly. But he reasoned the deputy wouldn't talk, being that he was Indian too, so he shut up for a while. Besides, the County Sheriff had figured out why the Indians laughed so frequently even though it wasn't as loud as it was before they were deputies.

Finally the law and the Indian deputies began to walk up Black Mesa. It's pretty steep and rough going up the mesa since it's really a mountain, not just a small mesa, and the deputies, who were still Indians, wouldn't say which was the best way to go. After a while the going was even rougher. One by one the real law dropped back to rest on a rock or under a piñon tree until only the Indian deputies were able to walk.

The deputies watched the Indian Agent sitting on a fallen log some yards back. He was the last one to keep up so far, and he was unlacing his shoes. The deputies waited patiently for the Indian Agent to start walking again and for the others to catch up.

"The weather is sure hot," one of the deputies said.

"Yes, but maybe it'll rain soon," another said.

"It rained last month for the last time this season," a third deputy offered.

"Then maybe next year," another said.

And looking back downtrail, the first deputy said, "Perhaps snow then."

They all watched the County Sheriff and the other police officer slowly walking toward them a half-mile back.

"Maybe the Mericano need a rest," a deputy said.

"Yes, they might need to rest," another said.

"I'll go tell that one we're going to stop and rest," another said and walked to where the Indian Agent sat on a log.

"We gonna stop to rest," the deputy said to the Indian Agent, who didn't say anything as he massaged his aching feet.

The Indians and the law didn't find Kaiser that day or the next day. The deputies said that they could walk for all eternity all over Black Mesa but they wouldn't find Kaiser. They said they didn't mind walking as long as they got paid for their time. Even the ones who weren't so sure about getting paid began to feel this way. Their corn crops were already in, and the cold weather wouldn't yet freeze the remaining pumpkins still out in the fields. And they'd just pay someone to haul winter wood for them now that they'd have the money.

And the deputies, who were still first of all Indian no matter what, still refused to talk. The ones who wanted to tell where Kaiser was, if they knew, didn't say so out loud. But they didn't tell, so it didn't make any difference. They were too persuaded by their newly found prosperity of employment.

By the middle of the second day of walking around a lot of Black Mesa, the exhausted County Sheriff had begun to sound like he was all for going back to Albuquerque. Maybe Kaiser would come in by himself. He didn't see any sense in looking for some Indian anyway, just to put him in the army. Besides, he'd heard the Indian was crazy. When the County Sheriff had first learned that the Indian's name was Kaiser, he couldn't believe it. He was assured that wasn't his real name though, just something he was called because he was crazy. But the County Sheriff didn't feel any better because of that assurance, and he was jumpy about the crazy part.

At the end of the second day, the law—which, like I said

before, was the County Sheriff, another officer, and the Indian Agent—decided to leave. "Maybe we'll come back. We'll have to talk this over with the Indian Affairs office. Maybe it'll be alright if that Indian doesn't have to be in the army after all." That's what the law said, although the County Sheriff, his six-shooter off his hip now, didn't say anything. He was about to collapse from weariness. And they all left.

The Indian Affairs office didn't give up, though. The officials, mainly office desk types who didn't have to walk a foot of Black Mesa, sent back more men, led reluctantly by the Indian Agent. The County Sheriff said it wasn't worth it because of his health. Besides, he had a whole county to take care of. The Indians were deputized again. This time more volunteered to be deputies, and many had to be turned away. They had figured out how to work it. They wouldn't have to tell if they knew where Kaiser was. All they would have to do was walk around and from time to time say, "Maybe Kaiser is over there by that red canyon. Used to be good hiding places around there back when the Apache and Navajo were raising hell." And some would go over that way, and some in another direction, investigating good hiding places.

But after camping around Black Mesa for a week, the Indian Affairs office gave up. This time even the Indian Agent was ready to call it quits or resign from the Indian Affairs office. But he and his men went by Faustin's home the day they left for Albuquerque and left a message. The message was that the government—in other words, the law—would wait, and when Kaiser least expected it the law would get him and he would go to jail.

Kaiser decided to volunteer for the army. He had decided after he had watched the law and the deputies walk all over the mesa. Grandfather Faustin had visited him up at one of the sheep camps.

The old man gave him all the news at home and told him about the government's search for him. And then he told Kaiser about the message the government law had left.

"Okay," Kaiser said. He was silent for a while, and then he nodded his head slowly like his grandfather would do in the midst of deep thought. "I'll join their army," Kaiser said.

Immediately the old man said, "No," loudly and strongly. "I don't want you to. I will not allow you."

"Grandfather, I do not have to mind you. If you were my grandfather or uncle on my mother's side, I would listen to you and probably obey you. But you are not, and so I will not obey you." That's what Kaiser said, saying it like he had thought about it quite a bit.

"You are really crazy then," Faustin said. "Mericano meh. If that's what you want to do, go ahead." The old man was angry. But he was sad too, and he stood up and put his hands on his grandson's shoulders and blessed him with prayer and counsel in the people's way.

Afterward, old man Faustin left. It was well into evening when he left the sheep camp where Kaiser was, and the old man walked a long time away from Black Mesa before he started to sing.

The next day, Kaiser showed up at home. He ate supper with us, and after we ate we all sat in the living room with my grandfather.

"So you've decided to go into the Mericano's army," my grandfather said to Kaiser, although he was also speaking to all of us in the room.

None of us kids nor even my parents had known Kaiser was going to do that, go into the Mericano's army, but my grandfather had known all along. He probably knew as soon as Kaiser walked into the house—maybe even before that.

Grandfather blessed him then with prayer and counsel, just like Faustin had done, and he talked to him of how a man should behave and what he should expect—general and significant things that Grandpa always said. He turned sternly toward us kids—who were playing around, not paying much attention, as usual—since it was important we should know those things too. My father and mother spoke too, and when they finished, Grandpa put cornmeal into Kaiser's hand for him to pray with. My father and mother told us kids to tell Kaiser goodbye, good wishes, and good health. After we did that, Kaiser left.

The next thing we heard was that Kaiser was in the state pen.

Later on, some people from the Pueblo went to visit him at the state pen. He was okay and getting fat, they said. He behaved and was getting on okay with everybody, the warden told them. When someone had asked Kaiser if he was okay, he said he was fine and he guessed he would be American pretty soon, being that he was around them so much. The people left Kaiser some home-baked oven bread and dried meat and came home after being assured by the warden that Kaiser would get out pretty soon, maybe right after the war. Yes, Kaiser was a model inmate, the warden added with a smile.

When the visitors got home to the Pueblo, they went and told Faustin his grandson Kaiser was okay, that he was happy and getting fat as any American. Old Faustin did not have anything to say about that.

Well, the war was over after a while. Old man Faustin died sometime near the end of it. Nobody had ever heard him mention

Kaiser at all. Kaiser's sister and nephew were the only ones left at their home. Sometimes when someone would ask about Kaiser, his sister or nephew would say, "Oh, he's fine. He'll be home pretty soon. Maybe right after the war ends." But after the war was over, they just said that Kaiser was fine.

My father and a couple of other guys went down to the Indian Affairs office to see what they could find out about Kaiser. It was sometime later, maybe it was a couple or several years later. They were told that Kaiser was going to stay in the pen longer now because he had tried to kill somebody. Well, he just went crazy one day, no reason; he made a mistake, so he'd just have to stay in for a couple more years or so. That's what the Indian Affairs said to my father and the other guys from the Pueblo.

That was the first anybody had heard of Kaiser trying to kill somebody. Some people said, Why the hell didn't they put him in the army for that like they wanted to in the first place? So Kaiser remained in the pen long after the war was over and most of the guys from the Pueblo who had gone into the army had come home. Eventually, though, when he was finally due to get out, the Indian Affairs sent a letter to the governor, and several men from the village went to get Kaiser to bring him home.

My father said Kaiser was quiet all the way home on the bus. Some of the guys tried to joke with him, but he just wouldn't laugh or say anything. When they got off the bus at the highway and began to walk home, the guys broke into song, but that didn't bring Kaiser around. He just kept walking quiet and reserved in his gray suit. One of the guys joked that Kaiser probably owned the only suit in the whole tribe.

"You lucky so-and-so. You look like a rich man," the joker said. The other guys looked at him sharply and he quit joking right away. But Kaiser didn't say anything. He just walked along very quiet.

When they reached home, Kaiser's sister and nephew were very happy to see him. They cried and laughed at the same time. But Kaiser didn't say or do anything except sit at the kitchen table and look around, although mostly he stared straight ahead. My father and the other guys gave him advice and counsel and welcomed him home again, and then they left.

After that, Kaiser always wore the gray suit. Every time you saw him, he was wearing it. Out in the fields or in the plaza watching the Kahtzina, he wore the suit. He didn't talk much anymore, and he didn't come around home anymore, either. The suit was getting all beat-up looking, my father said, but he just kept on wearing it, and some people began to say Kaiser was showing off.

"That Kaiser," they said, "he's always wearing his suit, just like he was an American or something. Who does he think he is, anyway?" And they'd snicker, looking at Kaiser with a sort of disdain. Or envy. Even when the suit was torn and soiled so that it hardly looked anything like a suit, Kaiser wore it. Some people said, "When he dies, Kaiser is going to be wearing his suit." They said that like they wished they had gotten a suit like Kaiser had.

Well, Kaiser died. But without his gray suit. He died up at one of his distant relatives' sheep camps one winter. When someone asked about the suit, they were told by Kaiser's sister that it was rolled up in some newspaper at their home. She said that Kaiser had told her, before he went to the sheep camp, that she was to send it to the government. But, she said, she couldn't figure out what he meant, whether Kaiser had meant the law or somebody else, maybe the state pen or the Indian Affairs office.

The person who asked about the suit wondered about Kaiser's

instructions. He couldn't figure out why Kaiser wanted to send a beat-up gray suit to the government. And then he figured, well, maybe that's the way it was when you either went into the state pen or the army and became an American.

The Way You See Horses

The boy and his father had taken two willow sticks and carefully split them. The willow wood was dry and very light but
not very strong. The boy's father took his pocketknife, tested the
blade's sharpness with his thumb, and split the sticks in half.

"I think they'll do," the father said.

"I hope they don't break," the boy said. He held one of the
sticks in his hand. It was so light he could barely feel its weight. He
felt its tension as he bent it into an arc.

"Be careful you don't bend it too far," his father said. He
notched the other stick a half inch from each end. That was for the
string.

They had gotten a plastic bag from under the kitchen sink
that morning. It was a heavy-duty trash bag—the kind that TV
advertisements say won't break even if a car engine is put in it—
and some tape to hold the plastic bag ends.

"Now," the father said, "we have the sticks, string, and plastic
bag, and all we need is a tail. And then we'll put it all together."

"What's the tail for, Dad?" the boy asked. He had seen tails on
kites before, but he didn't know what they were for.

"It's to keep one end, the bottom of the kite, weighed down
and upright. So it'll fly right," the father explained.

As they were putting the bag on the sticks and tying its string,
the wind picked up some. It gusted with sudden quick movements.
It billowed out the plastic bag so that the father had to hold one end

of the bag down with his knee while he trimmed the other end and began to fit it to the crossed form of willow sticks.

After several minutes, the wind quieted down and they soon finished the kite.

"Now we need a tail, don't we, Dad?" the boy said.

"Yeah, let's see what we can use," the father said. He picked up a strip of the plastic bag, but it was too light and he looked around some more. They were at the edge of a town park, and there didn't seem to be much of anything around.

He searched in his pockets and found a red flowered handkerchief. He bit an edge of the handkerchief and tore a narrow strip off. He cut several more strips until there wasn't anything of the handkerchief left.

His son watched him very closely.

"That's okay," his father said. "I've got another booger rag just like the other one." He smiled and ruffled the boy's hair.

"Booger rag," the boy said, and he giggled and squealed with laughter. "Booger rag!" He jumped up and down with delight, giggling.

The boy's father knotted the cloth strips together, and then he cut a bit of the string and tied the tail to the bottom of the kite.

"Now let's see what we have here," the father said grandly, holding up the kite they'd made. "Why, it's the genuine article, a real handmade kite. Here, Inspector, you want to pass inspection on it?"

The father handed the fragile-looking plastic-bag-and-willow-stick kite to the boy.

The boy held it in his hands and looked it over. The kite flapped some in a gust of wind. It felt alive, almost like a live animal or bird. The boy was smiling as his father tied the end of the ball of string to the kite.

"Now, you walk out a ways over that way," the father said. He pointed to the northeast in the direction the wind was blowing from.

"Just a minute, Son. Let's wait a bit until the wind goes down just a bit," the father said. "Otherwise, the kite might tear loose on us." They waited for several minutes.

"Okay. Okay, now. Hold it up," he told his son as the wind quieted down to a gentler pace. Standing next to his son, he held the ball of string.

And then he said, "Now. Now, let it go."

The boy let the kite go. It wobbled and kicked in the wind at the end of the string. His father fed out the string from the ball as he walked slowly in the direction the kite was flying. Soon, the kite was flying pretty high.

"Here, now you hold it for a while," the father said. "Keep the string taut, and give the kite more string once in a while." He held out the ball of string to his son.

The boy took the ball of string with both of his hands. The string vibrated in his hands and fingers. He could feel the kite jump and kick and tremble at the end of the string. It was like it was really alive.

The wind was powerful. The kite swung and made loops and half loops and sudden arcs. The sky was mostly blue, but there was a small mass of white clouds toward which the kite climbed.

"A bit taut now, Son," the father said. "Walk backwards a little." He walked backward himself, as if he held the kite string in his hand.

The father and son had moved yards away from where they had let the kite go toward the sky. The father watched his son watching the string inch from his hand, and he watched him turn his head toward the tumbling and gliding kite in the sky.

The Way You See Horses 41

The father suddenly felt the aching and desperate loneliness he often felt when he was alone someplace, when he would desperately wish he could be with his young son at that very moment.

The boy was intense with the kite. The kite jerked and then steadied and balanced perfectly in the sky. It was stopped dead still for just an instant before it jumped alive again.

The plastic-bag-and-willow-stick kite was at the edge of the outline of white clouds.

"Dad, the kite is going to hit the clouds," the boy shouted.

The boy's sudden loud voice startled his father, and boy and father locked glances for the briefest moment. The kite string was a thin, almost invisible line in the sky—but it was there, trembling, alive, and vibrating in the boy's hand. The father looked at the kite and the clouds.

"No, it won't hit," the father said. "The clouds are quite high. They're way over there." He indicated some hills toward the east.

The boy pulled back on the kite string anyway, and he walked backward a few steps. The kite looped and tumbled and it seemed to bump upon the clouds. The wind was quieter where the boy stood now. The string trembled in his hand.

"The clouds don't look far away," the boy said. And then after a quiet moment he said, "But they are." And he continued, "When you look at the kite and it's reflected against the clouds, it makes the clouds look like they're close. It's the way they look to you."

The father looked at the clouds again and at the kite. He watched the kite string vibrating in his son's small hand. He looked at his son. His son's eyes were lit with the depth of the blue sky and his boyhood.

Yes, of course, the father thought. That's the reason why the clouds look like they're so close. So close you could touch them. It's the way you see them.

There were horses in the sky. They moiled and tumbled into the shapes of their motions. They were playing. They were young — colts and mares and old studs. They thundered silently across the broad, flat plain of the blue sky. The horses were flying. The horses were trembling in the string the boy held in his hands. The boy could feel the bones, the eyes, the rippling muscle and skin, the power and the motion of the horses.

And the father could feel them in himself and in his son.

The father said, "The clouds are like horses. You can imagine horses in them. Can you see them?"

His son watched the clouds for several moments, and then he said, "Yeah. Yeah, Dad, I can see them. They're almost for-real horses. It's the same way the clouds seem to be real close, like my kite is touching them. It's the way you see them."

"Yeah," his father said. "It's the way you see them."

Feathers

The father and his son found the little black-and-white kitten in the alley behind the Grasshopper Bookstore. Its fur was so fluffy and unruly that it looked like ruffled feathers, and so they named it Feathers.

"Feathers. Come here, Feathers," the father said gently, urging the kitten to come to him as he held out his hands. "Don't you think that's a good name?" he said.

"He's got white circles around his eyes," his son said.

The father held the kitten gently in his hands. "It's kind of skinny. We should give it some food when we get back to the apartment." The kitten was several weeks old, maybe five weeks. It might be able to eat a bit of something.

They took Feathers to the boy's and mother's apartment. No one was there, and they sat down on the doorstep. "I wonder where your mother is," the father said.

"She might have gone shopping," the boy said. He cradled Feathers in his arms. He kept looking into the little kitten's eyes. It had very bright eyes, which were now about to close in sleep.

"I hope she lets you keep it," the father said. "Remember that little dog I brought you last summer? The puppy? She gave that away."

"The landlord didn't want pets around the apartments," the boy said, "so my mom gave it away."

"Maybe Feathers will be alright with the landlord. Kittens aren't much trouble," the father said.

The boy was very gentle with Feathers. He moved his hand very surely and carefully over the kitten, which had fallen asleep. "I think we'll need a box for its poop," he said, "with sand in it."

"Yeah, you'll need that. Cats got a lot of that," his father said, chuckling.

His son laughed, and he held the kitten away from him, just in case. Feathers' eyes fell brightly open.

Looking at his son, the father wondered how his son was coming along, how he was learning things. He loved his son who was now almost five years old. It was hard not to dwell too much on the pain of separation. He stroked the kitten with just the lightest touch of his fingertips.

"Maybe this summer you can come live with me for a while," the father said.

The boy did not say anything for a moment. And then, holding the kitten to his cheek, the boy said, "He's very warm. I can hear something inside of him."

"It's a she," his father said. "Feathers is a she, a girl kitten."

"Oh," the boy said. And then he said, "I'm going to enroll in a swimming class. My mother said I could. It's over at the university."

"You could still come and stay with me for a while," his father said.

At that moment, the boy's mother came home. She carried a couple of heavy grocery bags. "Hello," she said, looking only briefly at her ex-husband. There were sweat beads on her forehead.

The boy's father got up from the doorstep and said, "Let me help you." He held out his hands, offering to carry the grocery bags.

"No. That's alright. I'm doing okay," the boy's mother said. She fumbled for her house key in her shoulder bag. Finding it, she began to unlock the door.

Holding the heavy bags with one arm and leaning into the screen door to prop it open, she couldn't fit the key into the keyhole right away. The key fell to the cement doorstep with a flat tinkle.

"Here, I'll get it," the boy's father said. He picked up the key and fitted it into the door lock. And opened the door. He remembered very easily.

"David! Hold this screen door open. Don't just stand there like that," the boy's mother said. She stared fiercely at the black-and-white kitten snuggled in her son's arms. But only for a moment. And then she turned to enter their apartment.

Not knowing what to do, the boy's father stood uneasily at the door until he heard her call from inside. "Come in. It's so damned hot out there."

Stepping inside the apartment, he started to hang the house key on the nail on the wall, as he had done out of habit in another time, and then he decided not to. "Here's your key," he said to his ex-wife.

"Just hang it up," she snapped from the kitchen. "I'm trying to put stuff away. This house is a wreck." She banged things around in the kitchen.

Their son stayed outside. He had sat back down on the doorstep and continued to study the kitten. Feathers had gone to sleep again.

"We found a kitten. David, show the kitten to your mother," he said to his son through the screen door.

The boy's mother did not say anything, but she wasn't banging things around anymore.

David came into the apartment from outside. In a loud five-years-of-age voice, he said to his mother in the kitchen, "He's got white circles around his eyes. His name is Feathers." And then he remembered and said, "I mean she," his voice trailing away.

"It's a she kitten," his mother said, an edge in her voice. She came into the living room with a magazine in her hand. She looked at her ex-husband and studied him half a moment. She held out the magazine and said, "This has something of yours in it."

It was a regional travelogue type of magazine with gaudy color prints of Southwestern scenery. "I know," he said. "I saw it."

"Oh," she said, "I guess you would have." She flipped the magazine on an end table with other magazines.

It was a poem of his that was in the magazine. One day in late fall a couple of years before, they—mother, father, child—had driven into the mountains. They followed a road indicated on a map that showed that the road led across the mountains and down the other side. They had driven up the mountain on a gravel road which turned into a deeply rutted dirt road. And eventually the road became rougher and rougher until the ruts led nowhere. They were forced to turn around. There was no way they could drive over and through the mountains to the other side. On the way back after turning around, they had seen an old house. Only the old walls were standing. The walls were of stone, no mortar, just stone, and the stones were balanced against the blue sky so fragilely.

"I want to feed Feathers," David said to his parents. The kitten was waking up and stirring in the boy's arms.

"There's a little bit of tuna in a bowl in the refrigerator. Maybe she will eat a little of that. But the kitten's kind of small yet." The mother's voice had turned gentler.

"We found it behind the Grasshopper Bookstore," the father said. "It was in the alley. Maybe somebody abandoned it. Or lost it."

Their son brought a plastic bowl of stale tuna from the refrigerator. He set it down on the floor and put the kitten's nose to the tuna. Feathers ignored it at first, even turned away from it, and then she sniffed the tuna and sniffed it again. Finally, Feathers licked the tuna and began to gingerly nibble at it. She did it with tiny, deliberate nibbles.

The boy smiled and laughed happily. "Mom, Dad, look. He's eating, " he said with excitement. "Feathers is eating. He's eating the tuna! I mean she!" David squatted beside the kitten, and he looked with amazement at the kitten eating the food in the bowl.

Feathers did not pay any mind to being the center of attention focused on her by the mother, father, and son, who all watched her eating from the plastic bowl.

More than Anything
Else in the World

I t did matter. It mattered more than anything in the world.
Several days before, in San Diego, he had been walking in the
evening along the beach. A dog ran up to him and sniffed his knees
and pants cuffs. "Hello, puppy," he said. The German shepherd
looked up at his face, wagged its tail, then bounded off to join a
couple who waved to him.

There were lights out on the bay some distance from shore. It
was a boat or an offshore drilling rig. The lights bobbed up and
down. The horizon was metal and dark clouds. It was sometime
past sunset.

He knew that California was not for him. He knew that he
could live there but it was almost impossible for him. He had
known that for a long time. He had no doubt about this. But there
were things he always denied so strongly, the things he knew.

So he had boarded the eastbound bus the day before in San
Diego. Hours later, early, early in the morning of the next day, he
sat in the Phoenix bus depot. He tried to read a book of contempo-
rary American short stories. But the sentences and words in the
stories were just sentences and words. There was not a single story
in the paperback that rang familiar to him.

The sun was rising as the bus pulled into the parking lot of a
Howard Johnson's in Gallup, New Mexico. Pulling his denim

jacket snugly to him to ward off the cold March wind, he got out of the bus. He shivered. The sun was a weak orange bulb against a heavy gray sky.

On the cross-country bus out of Phoenix, he talked with a woman who sat in the seat beside him. He told her about the dog on the beach in San Diego. The woman was a French tutor in Albuquerque. At the Howard Johnson's breakfast stop, they found a table and continued their conversation.

"Ritual is important for me," he said to the woman. "I try to do certain things in the morning, hopefully not just methodically but meaningfully. I try to make them work meaningfully, anyway, in the ordinary scheme of things, make them an important part of what I do every day."

"My grandmother went to Catholic mass every morning," the woman said. "That was her ritual. Me? I don't do any. I go to the toilet, brush my teeth, comb my hair, fix toast and coffee. The usual things. They don't seem very important."

They ordered eggs, toast, and coffee when the waitress came to their table.

He watched a woman with long, dark hair sitting a couple of tables away. She wore a red dress and she had on a necklace of white shell that brought out the red vividly. He remembered his wife talking about a red dress.

After a moment of thought, he said, "I pray. Mostly I pray. It can be done anytime, anyplace. I need to." He remembered the desperate prayers on some mornings. He remembered his taut nerves tearing at the precarious mornings. He remembered the feathers clogged in his throat on those mornings. Sometimes ritual had nothing to do with it; prayer was simple necessity.

When the bus passengers had finished their breakfast, the bus loaded up again. It was the last stretch of the journey for him.

Then he would be back where he had begun just two months before. California was already a memory.

Just as the bus pulled into the regular downtown bus depot in Gallup, he looked out the bus window. An Indian woman was crossing the street near the depot.

Several Indian men followed her as she walked around to the side of a nearby building. She clutched a brown paper bag under her arm. She wore a sateen green blouse and a long skirt. The woman looked old, although she probably wasn't old. The weary lines in her face made her sadness and oldness sag.

The men gathered around her as she opened the paper bag and reached into it. From the bus windows, several people watched the ritual of the Indians. As he slouched down into his seat, he heard some passengers make snickering remarks.

It did matter. He had watched himself in the mirror of his memory. It was another person he saw, but it looked so much like himself that he could almost not bear to remember. He had searched every aspect of the image he saw and found himself looking frightened out of yellowed eyes.

"Of course it's important," the woman who was a French tutor said. "The learning process of a child is tied in completely with how the culture that he grows up in functions. A child cannot learn important values unless his culture lets him."

That wasn't what he had meant. He meant the Indian woman and the Indian men sucking at the wine bottle against the wall of a building next to the Gallup bus depot. He meant the escape from California. He had said, "Human beings learn from the pressures exerted on them. One's strength buckling under sometimes. That's the main learning process." That's what he meant.

The sun was rising into the midmorning sky as the bus journeyed eastward. Soon the bus would pass by the place where he had been a child. He closed his eyes and tried to sleep. The French tutor had dozed off and she leaned into him.

She smelled slightly sweaty and perfumed with some sweet scent. He tried to push her away without disturbing her, but she opened her eyes, looked at him, and smiled, and leaned closer into him. She was very warm.

Soon the bus passed by his home. He wanted to wake her and explain to her. But she was sound asleep and he didn't wake her. He looked and looked southward where his childhood had been spent. He looked and looked for a boy walking toward the gardens and fields that would be planted soon with spring seed.

When the woman awoke, she sighed and snuggled into him. Opening her sleepy eyes, she reached her hand for his, and closed her fingers around his hand. She held him gently and securely. "I had a dream," she said. "It was so warm and so . . . so comfortable."

He had been dozing, and he looked at her as she said that. He put his hand over hers. And he felt her movement toward him.

"Do you mind?" she said. She squeezed his hand.

"No," he said, shaking his head.

Later, when the bus pulled into the bus depot in Albuquerque, she said, "Come with me." She said it firmly, and she repeated, "Come with me."

"No," he said. He knew his wife didn't know he was coming home. He knew his wife didn't want him home. But he said no. It mattered more than anything else in the world that he say no.

Something's Going On

I

Nine-year-old Jimmo put on his new plaid shirt. He had been saving it since his latest birthday two months before. He had tried it on then, just to see how it looked. Willie, his father, had said, "Looks good," smiling proudly at his son, who was growing taller and stronger. Jimmo had taken off his new shirt, folded it carefully, and put it in the bottom drawer of the dresser he shared with his two brothers and a sister.

Jimmo straightened the collar of the new shirt and tucked the tails into his pants. He looked at himself in a round hand mirror he held before him. He couldn't see himself very well, so he propped the mirror on the rumpled bed and looked at himself with his new shirt. He wished they still had the big mirror his father had bought at the Sears in town as a surprise. The mirror had broken, though. His father had broken it.

Jimmo heard Albert and Perry, his two older brothers, laughing in the yard outside. He had been the last to get out of bed. Sleepy and tired, he had lain in bed, wishing it was still night. Not that night before, though, but some other night. His brothers had crawled over him and tried to get him up. But he wasn't ready to. Now, with his new plaid shirt on, Jimmo felt better.

His mother was busy in the kitchen. She was frying potatoes. Jimmo could smell them frying in lard. His mother had already called him once, and he knew that she would soon call him again.

When he went into the kitchen, she said, "You look very hand-some, Jimmo," but she could see that his face wore a look of worry and tiredness.

Jimmo rolled up his shirtsleeves and dipped cold water from a filled bucket into the washbasin. He dashed cold water on his face and soaped his hands. The soap smelled good, and he liked the feel of the pumice in the soap. His mother used that kind of soap because the boys did a lot of playing around in the dirt and at the village dump, where they weren't supposed to go but did. And it was the only soap that dissolved the oil and grease on the mechanic's hands of their father.

The boys used to bring home from the reservation school the soap that the federal government gave to the Indians. But Jimmo didn't like that soap because it smelled like the stuff the janitor used on the school floors. Jimmo's father said, "That's the stuff they use to clean toilet bowls." He replaced the government soap with little bars of scented soap he got from the gas station where he worked.

When Jimmo finished washing his face and hands, he combed his hair, but his stiff black hair still stuck up like a rooster's tail. He straightened his shirt collar and turned around for his mother to check him over. Jimmo wanted to look pleasing to her since he had been the last out of bed. His mother put the last tortilla on the stove to cook. With a big smile she said, "You're still looking fine, Jimmy-o." That was the name his father had called him when he was a toddler. And that was what his family used to call him until his little sister Santana began to call him Jimmo.

Jimmo smiled and tried not to let his tiredness show. Unable to sleep the night before, he had lain awake, listening to his mother moving around in the kitchen. Taking her time, she was curling her hair or something. He was surprised to see her doing that lately. His mother had worn her hair in braids for as long as he could remember, but now it was in curls.

After a long time had passed, Jimmo heard the refrigerator door open and shut when his mother put away the supper food left out for his father. He heard her turn off the kitchen light. A hard lump was curled into a knot in Jimmo's throat. He smothered his sobs, because he didn't want his brothers to call him a crybaby.

"We're ready to eat. Call your brothers and sister," Jimmo's mother said to him. Jimmo went outside. Albert and Perry were pushing Santana in a little wagon they had salvaged from the village dump. Santana squealed with delight and made loud motor sounds like her older brothers. Jimmo ran up and tried to jump on the wagon to ride with Santana.

"Get off, Jimmo. Get off! Go'wan!" Albert shouted.

"You're too big for the wagon," Perry said. The older brothers pushed Santana in a circle around a tree.

"Wait! Stop!" Santana's voice was loud. In fact, she was louder than all her brothers put together. Santana was tiny, but for a little kid she had the loudest yell in the village. "Stop!" she yelled again. "Come on, you can ride with me," she said to Jimmo.

"Come on, Jimmo! Come on!" Santana urged loudly. Albert and Perry didn't say anything as Jimmo climbed into the wagon and they were off again. Santana clung tightly with her little hands around Jimmo's stomach as they went around and around the tree. One of the boys stumbled and fell, and they were all laughing when their mother called them to eat breakfast.

II

After the breakfast dishes had been washed and put away, they walked to Sunday mass. Albert and Perry ran ahead, and Jimmo and Santana walked with their mother. Although it was October and there had been snow at the beginning of the month, it wasn't cold now. The sun was shining brightly. Her little hand in her mother's hand, Santana walked as fast as she could, but at times her mother had to slow down for her.

"Mama, look at the mountain. There's more snow," Jimmo said.

He pointed at the mountain peaks to the west from which clouds were now thinning away. She looked and nodded her head. Thinking of snow and wind, she shivered, her thoughts on how cold the weather might soon become.

"Do you remember we made a snowman last year with Daddy?" Santana said. Santana had cut a picture of a snowman from a magazine and had shown it to her father. He looked at it and said, "That's some fancy snowman. Hmmmm. Okay, let's make one of our very own!"

He dressed Santana warmly, and the boys put on their coats and ran into the fresh snow to make their own snowman.

At first they tried to find things that would make their snowman look like the one in the magazine picture. But they didn't have a carrot for the nose or coal for the eyes or a straw hat. But colored broken glass worked alright, and their father fashioned a big brown nose out of a bar of government soap. The last thing they did was prop a set of old VA hospital crutches under the arms of the snowman.

Albert, Perry, Jimmo, and Santana had great fun making their very own snowman, which they called Daddy. They called their mother to come see Daddy the Snowman. Their mother giggled and said it was silly, and she was happy for her growing children and her husband Willie.

Skipping as she walked, Santana said, "It's fun to walk. It's fun to walk, isn't it, Mama?" Her mother squeezed her hand and smiled at her youngest child.

Usually Jimmo thought walking was fun too, but he was tired and groggy from lack of sleep. Sometimes his father drove them in the truck to Round Point. The children would walk and run, and it was fun then. Even though he had to use crutches because of his missing leg, their father could almost keep up with their running. Sometimes his crutches would suddenly sink into the sand and trip him, but he had a good sense of balance and most of the time he wouldn't fall.

Once Jimmo had watched his father making his way up a distant hill. He had watched him slowly make his way up the hill on his crutches. When he reached the top of the hill, his father seemed to be on the verge of walking into the sky.

Jimmo had hollered loudly, "Daddy, wait!" And he had run as hard as he could to reach his father. Hearing Jimmo's holler, his father had turned and watched his son running toward him. When Jimmo reached his father, he hugged him as hard as he could.

On another occasion, they had looked for oak from which their father wanted to make new crutches. They looked for just the right size and straightness of oak limb. Finally in a canyon, they came upon a stand of oak brush. The oak limbs were thin and straight. Their father ran his hands carefully up and down their length, feeling their strength. He chose several limbs that he would shape into crutches.

"This one," he said.

And then he took some cornmeal knotted within a handker-chief out of his shirt pocket and placed some of the meal in each of his children's hands.

"You must always do this first," he said.

The father and children prayed with their appreciation for the oak, the earth, the sun, their lives, and all things. He motioned for his children to follow along, to breathe upon the cornmeal, giving it life so life would continue. After they sprinkled the living food upon the stand of oak brush, Albert used the axe skillfully and soon cut the selected oak for his father.

When the children and their mother arrived at the church, mass was about to start. The boys wanted to sit in the back pews, so Jimmo and his brothers found a pew and crowded into it, shoving and pushing each other and causing a man to glare at them sternly. Albert and Perry didn't like to sit still for very long, but the boys managed to be quiet for a while.

When it was time for communion to be received, Jimmo watched people making their way to the altar railing. The priest and an altar boy came before the row of kneeling people and served the host upon the tongues of the people. The nuns said it was the body of Jesus, who was God, that was in the host. Jimmo tried to imagine God in the host when the priest held aloft the thin white wafer, but he never managed to see Him. He watched his mother as she made her way to the railing in a line of people with clasped hands and downcast eyes.

Jimmo had seen his father making his way through the crowded aisle. With his crutches, his walk was jerky and awkward and he would often come to a halting stop. In the fields and pas-tures and mesa meadows, his movements were smooth and fluid, but in church they were stumbly and slow. Eventually reaching the railing, he would lean his crutches aside and kneel with his one knee. After receiving the host, he'd retrieve his crutches and make his way back to the pew.

When the priest spoke about "our crippled and maimed in the recent war and those less fortunate than we who are whole in body and spirit," Jimmo began to worry again. Jimmo tried to concentrate on the quiet in the church when the priest's words focused on how people must understand that burdens were placed on them by the will of God. Jimmo tried to understand how it all fit together, but he could only envision a jumbled succession of vague impressions: God, host, burden, crutches, his father.

The knotted ache in Jimmo's throat came back. He tried to swallow the lump into his chest. Even though he didn't exactly understand what God was, he was about to agree to the will of God when Perry poked him in the ribs. He and Albert were giggling. They usually came to a point when they couldn't stand the mass. They'd giggle about anything remotely funny. Jimmo welcomed the interruption, but the people in front of them pointedly whispered for them to be quiet. Undeterred, the boys continued to exchange half-glances while they looked straight ahead at the slow-motion movement of the mass.

As soon as mass was over, the boys pushed through the crowd into the sunlight and fresh air outside. People stood around in small groups. Elders talked tribal politics and about their livestock and community activities. "No one ever wants to do community work for the people anymore," someone would say. "Yes, that's very true," several would agree.

Younger men and boys sat on a large pine log in the church-yard, and they leaned on their family pickup trucks and talked in quiet laughing voices. They eyed Sunday-dressed girls and flirted with them. The women laughed and gossiped, and sometimes they cried onto each other's shoulders. A relative had gotten hurt in an accident or was gravely ill, and another was having trouble again with her daughters and sons. "These days are very hard, sister," a woman would say. "That's true, that's true," others would sympathize. "You have to be strong, like a woman, and have courage. That's the only way."

Jimmo listened to an aunt talk with his mother. She asked, "How is my brother Willie? I didn't see him in church this morning." With a stammer in her voice, his mother said, "He's well but his leg has been hurting him lately."

"Has he been staying home?" the aunt asked. She probed for the reply she had in mind.

"Yes, yes," his mother said. "But he didn't come home last night. I don't know where he is right now."

Jimmo winced. He wished his aunt would leave his mother alone. Trying to share some of his young strength, Jimmo straightened himself as tall as he could and stood close to his mother. He was silently furious with his mother, and he grew impatient with some women relatives who joined them.

"Your uncle Santiago saw Willie driving on the old road towards Cebolla last evening. He thought he saw him turn into that Mexican bar there," one of the women said. "You poor sister," another relative said. "The only way is to be strong and have courage." She whimpered and dried her eyes with the edge of her shawl.

Jimmo was glad when they left for home, but he was unhappy when his aunt offered them a ride in her truck. When Jimmo's mother asked where Albert and Perry were, Santana said they had already left for home. A distance away, they saw Albert and Perry walking along the road. When they stopped for the boys, Albert said they didn't want to ride. Jimmo envied his brothers' defiance, and he wished he could get out and walk with them.

When they got home, while his mother busied herself with cleaning the house, Jimmo noticed fresh truck tire tracks in the yard. His father's truck tires! At first, Jimmo thought he was mistaken, but when he studied the tracks closely he knew he was not mistaken. Jimmo's heart quickened, and questions ran through his mind: Where could he have gone? Where is he? Why didn't he stay? He ran around the other side of the house, searching the roads leading into the distance. Nothing was in sight. He ran to tell his mother about the tracks.

"Yes, your father must have been here," his mother said quietly. She was standing by a wall closet. "His Levi coat is gone." Jimmo felt shock, his tension suddenly acute. There were little bursts in his chest.

Santana, standing by her mother, began to cry. "Shut up, crybaby," Jimmo said to her in a hard whisper, trying to relieve his own fear and confusion. His little sister continued to sob.

In an anguished cry, Jimmo asked, "But where is he? Where did he go?"

With a heavy sigh, his mother said, "I don't know, Son." She hugged Santana to her.

When Jimmo went into the room he and his brothers shared, he stared all around. The boys had helped their father build the room. They had helped him to measure, saw, and nail. Jimmo was looking at a wooden cabinet they had made when he heard a car drive into the yard. It was followed by another car, which drove around to the other side of the house and stopped. When Jimmo took a quick look inside the cabinet, he saw his father's .30–30 hunting rifle was gone. A cry of dismay escaped from him.

III

The thump of heavy footsteps and voices led Jimmo into the kitchen. The tribal governor was standing before Jimmo's mother. The man was uncomfortable and he took deep breaths as he paced his words. "Sister, I've come to see my brother Willie. These policemen have come with me to see him also. They want to talk with him."

"He is not here," Jimmo's mother said. "Why do the Mericano policemen want to talk with Willie?" she asked, her voice trembling.

Jimmo stood frozen, his breath thin and tense. Santana clung tightly to her mother's skirt. In English the governor spoke to the two white state policemen, who stood towering over him. He said, "She wants to know why you want to talk to her husband Willie."

"Dammit, you know why we want to talk to him," the older policeman said impatiently. The other was looking over the room, his eyes scanning all around. He looked nervous and his nose was slightly wrinkled. "Tell her what I told you," the policeman said to the governor.

"Sister," the governor said to Willie's wife, "the reason these policemen have come to talk with Willie is that over at the place where Willie works, something has happened."

"What has happened?" she asked. Her voice was shallow and strained, like she didn't want to ask the question.

"Mr. Glass, the owner of that gas station and garage, is dead. There were signs of violence. It appears that someone killed him.

Mr. Glass was found this morning. That's why they want to talk to my brother Willie." The governor nodded to the policemen, indicating he had told her.

Jimmo saw his mother's eyes flash with anger and fear at the Mericano policemen, but he could also see them well with tears.

"I don't know where Willie is," she said to the governor. She spoke in their native Indian language. "Your brother was not home last night."

Jimmo wanted to tell his mother to stop talking, but he couldn't talk or move. It was like he was frozen still.

His mother's voice continued. "The children and I came home from church just a while ago. Willie wasn't here. He must have been here while we were at mass, because his heavy coat is gone. And he took some food." She pointed to the bread box and an empty plate which had held food meant for him the night before.

In English the governor spoke to the white policemen. "She says he was here."

"Was!" the older policeman said loudly. "Was! Where is he now? Did she talk to him?"

"No, she didn't talk with him. She and the children were at church. She thinks he came home while they were at church. And then he left. He ate some food." The governor spoke quietly and pointed at the empty plate on the kitchen table.

As if they might see how Willie sat there eating, the policemen looked at the table. "Let's look around the place," the younger policeman said.

For a moment it was quiet until Santana began to wail loudly. Her mother gently stroked her head.

"He's gone," the older policeman said. He said to the governor, "Ask her if she has any idea where he went."

After the woman listened to the question asked by the governor, she said in Indian, "Where? I don't know, brother." She repeated "I don't know" quietly, murmuring rather than speaking, shaking her head.

"She doesn't know," the governor said to the policemen, who looked at him distrustfully.

"Does she know whether he's been acting strange lately? Whether he and Glass were on bad terms? You know, arguing, stuff like that." The policeman had a hard edge in his voice.

The governor cleared his throat. He didn't like to be doing this, probing for the kind of answer the police wanted. During his term of tribal office there had never been this kind of trouble. The governor told the woman what the police wanted to know.

"Do the Mericano policemen think Willie killed Mr. Glass?" Jimmo's mother asked, looking directly into the governor's face.

"Yes, that's what they believe," the governor said. They continued to speak in their native tribal language. "Maybe there was a fight. Glass is dead. They're looking for information. But they suspect Willie did it. That's why they came to find Willie. So they can talk with him."

Speaking calmly and with somewhat more assurance, Willie's wife said, "It's not definite then, that Willie did it?"

"No," the governor said. "They don't know for sure. That's only what they think."

With a stern look at the Indians, the older policeman asked, "What's she saying?" He did not like for them to be talking in a language he didn't understand.

"She says she doesn't know," the governor answered simply and firmly.

The policeman glared at the governor, not trusting him at all.

"What do you mean, she doesn't know? Doesn't she talk to her husband? Doesn't he talk about his job with Mr. Glass?" His voice bristled with impatience.

Jimmo wanted to tell them his father sometimes talked like he hated Mr. Glass. Jimmo wished the cops would leave them alone.

"What did your husband take? Did you notice anything? Do you have any idea where your husband went?" The younger policeman spoke to Jimmo's mother in loud, aggressive English, although he didn't know if she understood English.

Although she did not speak English very often, she didn't falter as she said, "No. I don't know." Her face was firmly set and her eyes stared straight back at the policeman.

"He took some food and his coat," the governor added, nodding at the woman to indicate that's what he had learned from her.

Furious with anger, Jimmo shouted silently at the cops: My father took his deer rifle! I hope he shoots you with it!

"Let's go," the older policeman said, and they turned to leave.

When the police had gone out the door, the governor said, "It is not definite that Willie did anything wrong. They only speculate. For now, they want to know where he is so they can talk with him." Speaking in their native language, his voice was gentle and reassuring.

"Yes, brother, I understand you," the woman said. "But you know how Willie talks, the things he says about the Mericano and their ways. He is always talking like that."

"That's true," the governor agreed. "I have heard him. That's the way Willie talks. It's true, as you know. The things he says, many of those things are true. That is what has happened and what has happened to us, what they have done."

Listening to the governor speak in the deliberate manner of

their people, Jimmo felt more reassurance now than when the governor talked in English to the police.

"You must conduct yourself as the strong woman you are. If it is true Willie did anything wrong, then it is up to his conscience and the Great Spirit. Only he and the Great Spirit know. We must believe in the strength and courage given to us by the Great Spirit of life. Have faith and ask for help from the Great Spirit, who knows and is able to help us."

The governor turned to the children huddled together.

"My beloved sons and daughter, you must be helpful to your mother and your father. They have both suffered. They need help, just like we all need help. Ask the Great Spirit for help. It is only the Great Spirit who is able to give us strength and courage." He stepped forward and put his arms around all of them for a moment. Then he turned for the door and left.

As soon the governor stepped outside, the older state policeman asked him, "You know if these are Willie's truck tracks?" He pointed to the tracks freshly made by snow tires.

"Yes," the governor said, nodding his head. Willie drove a ten-year-old pickup truck, and the governor knew it could get around pretty good in the mesas and hills above the village and even farther back on the mountain beyond.

"He'll just have to be hunted and tracked down, looks like," the younger policeman said. He looked at the house and at the yard, trying to note things that might help with finding Willie.

"You think Willie Bear killed Mr. Glass?" the governor asked quietly. The older policeman looked at him. Then, averting his gaze, he said, "If you ask me personally, I think that Indian probably did. I know about that Indian." He patroled the area bordering the reservation, and he knew some of the Indians in the community. "I threw him in jail a couple of times," he said to his younger partner, his tone of voice like a warning.

Later, when the Indian tribal police arrived, Jimmo's mother told them Willie must have come home while she and her children were at church and had taken his coat and some food. One of the tribal police asked if he had taken anything else.

Although not wanting to, she went into the boys' room to check the cabinet, but before she looked Jimmo said, "The rifle is gone."

She looked in the cabinet and saw the rifle was not there.

She told the tribal policeman, who said, "I hoped Willie wouldn't do anything like that. Looks like he's gone off somewhere. We better get going." He didn't like to think of going after one of their own people. "Willie will be alright," he said to Willie's wife.

Not knowing what to do, Jimmo opened the cabinet again. The cabinet held hunting and fishing gear. There was a .22 rifle for rabbits and an old shotgun for ducks. There was a hunting vest made by their father from old blue jeans. Even though he used crutches because of his missing leg, their father would take his sons hunting, even in the snow.

Sometimes he'd slip and fall, but usually they'd just laugh about it. The older boys always carried the gun, and their father would say things like "Always be very careful with guns," "Don't cross the fence with the gun in your hand," "Check your safety," and "Take a slow, deep breath and squeeze."

He'd tell the boys hunting stories from when he was younger. He would say, "When it was deer season, men and boys would go hunting together. But before they went hunting, they made careful preparations. Hunting songs and prayers were part of their preparations. They made and painted sacred sticks so they would be successful in their hunt, so they would be able to beckon the deer to them, and so the deer would gladly come to the village with them. It was always very carefully done in the old days. Now, although it isn't exactly like it was in the old days, you must always do the best you can."

Their father sang hunting prayer songs. "This is the song the hunter sings when he wants the mountain lion to turn the deer toward him." And he would say, "This is what you're to do because a long time back this is what was done. This is what the people of the old times did. Always remember this." And the boys sang along with their father when he sang the songs.

One fall, Albert, the oldest, went hunting with his uncles. He returned home full of stories about how the hunters went into the mountains and how their uncles had gotten their deer. Perry and Jimmo envied their older brother Albert, and their father promised the boys they would go hunting too, perhaps the next year.

Now Jimmo thought about all this as he tried to remember the songs his father sang. But he was confused, tense, and afraid, and he worried about his father's safety.

When evening came, the governor and two tribal elders came to their home. The governor said, "The Mericano police are convinced Willie killed that man Glass. They're not looking for anyone else. They say they have proof. They say there is a witness who saw what happened."

When Willie's wife was silent, the governor went on. "The state police say they know the things Willie used to say, the way he talked, that he didn't like the Mericano. They are going to look for him until they find him. That's what the policemen say." Willie's wife still did not say anything, so the governor continued. "I'm not convinced Willie did anything. Is there really someone who saw what happened? Maybe it was another Mericano." And then as if he were thinking aloud, the tribal governor said, "But why didn't my brother Willie stay when he came home?"

Finally, Willie's wife spoke. "Willie talks the way he does, but I don't know what he is thinking. I ask him why he talks like that. What is the matter? Why are you talking like that? He talks, but I don't know what he is thinking. He says the Mericano are against us. Willie talks, but I don't know what he is thinking. Perhaps I do not understand. And perhaps I do not want to know."

When Jimmo heard his mother saying this to the governor and the elders, he could hear his father talking. He had heard him say, in a grave and serious tone of voice, "I do not want you to be afraid, but something's going on."

Jimmo had not understood. The word "something" had stood out like a big shadow. He thought "something" had to do with his father's missing leg or his fear and anger. But Jimmo didn't know. Or perhaps he didn't want to know. "Something's going on," Jimmo could hear his father saying.

"They're after us. For a long time, they've been after us. They're after this land, this house, and even the Old Place. Yes, they're after the Old Place." Jimmo's father meant the old village where the people had first lived and built their homes. "They haven't taken enough yet. Not even when they are rich and power-ful. Not even with their cities and highways and airplanes. They want more. They want our hearts, our spirits, our lives. They are so empty. They are so hungry. They believe they can stop their hunger by filling themselves with what we have."

A vague yet recognizable real feeling made Jimmo vastly apprehensive when he heard his father talk like that. His father's words were full of anger and pain and fear. His father would be livid with rage, but there was something Jimmo did not understand—and he felt perhaps even his father did not understand. Yet Jimmo struggled to understand because if he did not understand, the powerful dread would rise uncontrollably and swallow them up.

Now one of the elders who had come with the governor spoke. "The people of Buck Well are talking about coming to look for our son. That man Glass was well-liked. They say an Indian has no right to harm an American. They say that Glass was good to Indians, so why should one of them have killed him? I don't know personally how good he was, but I know some of our people did not like him much." The other elder nodded his head in agreement.

"Glass was with the state government," the governor said. "His relatives are the trading post owners at Cebolla. When the law to allow state police to come onto the reservations was being discussed, he was for the law. He made speeches about how the law would protect us. During Christmastime, he brought gifts to the Indian children at school. "

"He was always expecting much from Willie," the other elder said. "They argued about Mericano people and Indian people. Glass would get very angry and call Willie and our people unsavory names. Willie told me he did not like working for Mr. Glass. I asked him why he did not stop working for Mr. Glass. 'Where can I get another job?' he said. It's true about the way Willie felt about the Mericano. I've felt that way too."

When the elders stopped talking, Jimmo's mother asked the tribal governor the question she had asked him before. "It's not definite that my husband, Willie, who is the father of my children, is responsible for what happened?"

"That's true," the governor said, "but the Mericano people of Buck Well believe he is responsible. Since they moved to that land area where one of the Old Places is, we have never gotten along with the Mericano. That is a matter our grandparent elders talked about, and it goes back to a time long ago. That is what we have to think about when the Mericano begin to talk about coming to look for Willie."

After a brief pause, the governor went on in a firmer voice. "We spoke against the law the Mericano wanted to make. That law would permit them to come onto our land whenever they pleased. Even now, even without that law, the state policemen have come asking for Willie. What we need is a law that protects us from the Mericano!" The governor's voice was especially strong and angry at the end.

As Jimmo listened to every word his elders spoke, he visualized the Mericano of Buck Well who wanted to hunt and find his father. He heard one of the elders say, "One of my sons says that when our young men go into Buck Well, they get beat upon by groups of them. The whites force them into fights, cursing them, calling them indecent names, and pushing them until someone gets hurt, like that boy who lost an eye last year."

As the governor and elders were leaving, the tribal sheriff arrived. "The Buck Well people are talking crazy and wild. I told them we would find Willie and take him to Buck Well, but they won't listen. They say we won't do it. They say that, because we're Indians, we won't do it. The state and county police are with them. They're not saying anything to stop the people of Buck Well. All of the Mericano are together in this. They say one of Willie's crutches was found covered with blood. I left to come tell you what they are saying."

Santana had fallen asleep on her mother's lap. Her brothers were red-eyed and dazed. Jimmo had a huge lump in his chest and throat. He wanted to beg the men to protect his father from the people of Buck Well, but he felt that they, too, were becoming convinced his father had done the killing. And he felt that even if they thought Willie's reason for doing it was justified, they wanted him to face up to it. Because of this, they would ultimately not help him.

The governor, the elders, the tribal sheriff, and the others would not protect Willie. And they could not prevent the Buck Well people from doing what they wanted to do. Jimmo realized that what his father talked about would swallow them up. "Something's going on," his father said. Although the people would know then what it was they dreaded and that it was swallowing them up, they would not be able to prevent it. Something was going on.

Before the governor left, he said, "Pray to the Great Spirit to help us. Our men will help and do what they can to protect Willie."

Jimmo heard his words, but he did not believe him. He saw that the men were cautious and frightened, and the burden of their fear was more convincing than their declarations of help for his father. It had been going on for too long. It was said that strength and courage came from the Great Spirit when you asked for help, but Jimmo found it difficult to believe. He felt that if help came, it would come only when the people truly became strong and courageous. Instead of merely saying "We are a people," the people would have to make a stand for what that meant.

Later, as Jimmo was falling asleep, a memory came to him like a dream. *His father was speaking: One of the great-grandfathers was a warrior. He fought against their army. Many of the people believed nothing could be done when their army came. He would go into their camp at night and chase their horses away and destroy what the army used against the people. They called him a thief and an outlaw. Some of our people even called him that, but he fought when others did not. The army caught the warrior. They put him in chains. They beat him and were going to hang him. He said, "Go ahead and kill me. That is the way you do things and you call it right."*

Finally some of our people went and talked with the warrior. They told him they wished for him to give up his actions, that it was best to get along with the Mericano father in Washington. The great-grandfather warrior said to the men who were elders, "I respect and honor you, because you and my grandfathers are the only true elders we have. I cannot do what the army of the enemy people tell me to do, but I will do what you want me to do." The elders got the warrior's release on the condition that he go to school in the East. He was sent to the East, where his warrior's hair was cut. Eventually though, after attending school in the East for a while, he left the school and returned home and farmed his fields until he became an old man and died. By the time he returned to his home, the Mericano army had left. Jimmo fell asleep within the memory-dream.

IV

It was still dark and very early in the morning when Jimmo awoke. He knew he must go and help his father. He knew he must hurry and find him before the people of Buck Well did. Jimmo wanted to wake his brothers to tell them of his decision, but he was afraid they would try to change his mind.

Jimmo dressed as quickly as he could. He took the .22 rifle from the cabinet and a box of shells. In the kitchen he wrapped some tortillas in an empty flour sack to take with him. When he opened the door to leave, he made sure he didn't make a sound.

The early morning was cold, and frost lay on the ground. Intuition led him toward the mesa above the village and the mountain beyond. He knew he had to hurry, and he began to run. Cold air stung his lungs, and he slowed to a walk from time to time. Jimmo remembered his father saying that they ran to the mountaintop and back in a few hours. Jimmo had wondered if they had wings or magical power to carry them as swiftly as the wind. They had songs, his father said. Their running and songs became a prayer for strength, endurance, and courage.

When Jimmo began running again, he began to sing. Each running step was a sound and a syllable in the song. The wind came into the song. And the morning came into the song. And this became the prayer of his running. Jimmo soon came to know the prayer of his running and singing. And this prayer became his purpose and reason and strength and endurance and courage as he ran toward the mountain.

In the early morning darkness, Jimmo's footsteps were guided by the prayer-song, and he soon arrived at the foot of the mesa. Climbing as fast as he could, Jimmo got to the top just as dawnlight was beginning. Full daylight would soon break over the eastern horizon. After catching his breath for a moment, he went on.

The light of the rising sun brought a fuller awareness to Jimmo than he had before. As his thoughts became more focused and clearer, he asked himself where exactly was he going. He tried to remember if his father had mentioned something or someplace about where he was to go. When Jimmo couldn't remember, doubt crept into his resolve and even though he could see where his footsteps fell, he was unsure of where to go.

He climbed a crevice in the sandstone walls of the mesa cliffs, and he was in a piñon forest now. Except for his hard breathing, a cold wind blowing toward him was the only sound he heard.

Jimmo knew the mountain was beyond the mesa forest, and he began to run again. Soon his chest ached from his exertion and he slowed to a walk. He stumbled to a log to catch his breath.

As Jimmo rested, the reason for why he had come in this direction suddenly came to him. It was because of the story of the warrior his father told. Stories were sometimes difficult to remember because some were long and full of detailed events and experiences. But Jimmo tried very hard to remember the warrior's story. Before he was caught, the warrior, who was called an outlaw even by some of his own people, had hidden on the mountain. He had gone to an Old Place where their ancestral people had lived. It was a place with homes carefully built into the canyon walls of the mountain. Pine trees stood nearby, and clear water ran in the canyon stream. And it was to this Old Place, his father said, that runners went with their prayers because of the sacred shrine that was there.

Jimmo knew then where he was going, because he remembered the story. And he remembered the direction told in the story. Jimmo and his brothers and little sister and their father had traveled in that direction when they were looking for oak limbs for their father's crutches. With excitement stirring new energy in him, Jimmo realized where he was going now. He was going toward the home of the ancestral people and the sacred shrine on the mountain.

Soon Jimmo arrived at the canyon at the foot of the mountain. It was the canyon in which they had found the oak grove. Sliding and leaping from boulder to boulder, Jimmo descended the canyon. He followed the winding road along the canyon floor until he came to the oak grove.

Jimmo saw that his father had been there. His truck tracks were clearly imprinted on the ground. He saw also that his father had been using only one crutch. So his father had come to the oak grove to get another limb for a crutch. But then Jimmo suddenly discovered the other crutch. The crutch was standing carefully upright within the oak thicket, just as if it had grown there— although the crutch was shiny with use and had no bark. Jimmo was bewildered. Looking around, he asked, How could Daddy have gone on without a crutch? Is he someplace nearby? Jimmo frantically searched the oak grove with his gaze. Daddy, where are you?

The pickup truck was nowhere in sight, so Jimmo realized his father must have driven farther into the mountain. He knew that eventually the road climbed out of the canyon and onto the mountainside. Jimmo found a fresh oak stump where his father must have cut a limber cane with which to walk. Searching the ground, Jimmo saw that the one-legged footprints his father made did not appear uncertain. Where the oak growth was freshly cut, he imagined his father standing on his one leg as he prayed for the strength and courage he needed.

Jimmo now prayed too as he stood with his hand on Willie's discarded crutch, which had become an oak in the growing earth again. And softly, easily, gently, Jimmo began to cry. He trembled with humility and the realization of his part among all things in the universe, and he trembled with the decision he had made. And because Jimmo recognized that this was his prayer, he was relieved and rested and stronger. Jimmo took a deep breath. He knew now where his father was going. And he knew he was to follow.

The Killing of a State Cop

Felipe was telling me how it happened. I was then twelve years old. He knew they would get him, he said. And he was scared. He looked around nervously all the time we sat on the trough that ran around the water tank.

Felipe wasn't a bad guy. Not at all. A little wild maybe. He had been in the Marines, and he could have gotten kicked out if he had wanted to, he said. But he hadn't because he could play it pretty straight like a good guy too.

He used to tell me a lot of things, about what he'd seen, about what he had done, about what he planned to do, and about what other people could do to you. That was one trouble with him. He was always thinking about what other people could do to you. Not the people around our place, the Indians, but other people.

How that state policeman died was like this. Felipe wanted me to always remember what he said. He talked very seriously, and sometimes sadly, and again he said they would get him anyway.

"What the hell, he deserved to die, the bastard."

It was the wine, Felipe said. And that thing he had about people, I guess. He didn't say, but I knew.

"It makes you warm in the head and other things like that," he said.

He had gone to town from the reservation with Antonio, his brother. They drove their pickup truck to town, where they bought the wine from a bootlegger. "From some stupid Mexican bartender. Geesus, I hate Mexicans."

Felipe spat on the ground. Indians were not supposed to drink or buy liquor at that time. It was against the law. Felipe hated the law and broke it whenever he felt he could get away with it.

"One time in Winslow," Felipe said, "I got off the train when it stopped at the depot and walked into a bar next to the depot to buy a beer. I was still in the Marines then and in uniform. This barman, he looked at me very mean and asked if I was Indian. 'Shore,' I said. And he told me to get the hell out before he called the cops. Goddamn, I hated that, and I went around the back and peed on the back door. I don't know why, just because I hated him I guess."

Felipe and his brother were walking in town, not saying anything much, maybe looking at things they wanted to buy when they had the money. They stopped in front of the Golden Theater and looked at the pictures of what was at the movies that day and the next day.

"Hey, Indio. What the hell you doing?" It was Luis Baca, a member of the state police who patrolled the state highway near the reservation.

The brothers hated the man. Felipe regarded him with a fierce hatred because he had been thrown in jail by him once. He had been beaten, and he feared the cop because of that. The brothers did not answer.

"Hey, goddammy Indio, get the hell away from there. Get out of town."

For no reason at all.

"For no reason at all. Goddamn, I got mad, and I called him a dirty, fat, lazy, good-for-nothing, ugly Mexican."

Felipe looked around and told me I better learn to be something more than him, a guy who would probably die in the electric chair up at Santa Fe.

Felipe told Antonio he was going to kill the Mexican, but Antonio said that it was no good talk and persuaded him to leave town.

The brothers left, followed by the curses and jeers of Luis Baca. When they got back to the pickup truck, they opened another bottle of wine and drank.

"It makes a noise in your head, and you want to do something," Felipe told me.

The brothers decided to go home. Almost out of town, they heard a siren scream behind them and saw a black police car with Baca driving it. Felipe told Antonio not to stop. They did not go faster, though. Luis Baca drove alongside them and laughed at the brothers, who were frightened and suspicious.

Antonio stepped on the brake then, and he let the policeman pass them. They were past the town limits.

"Antonio, my brother, he is kind of a funny guy," Felipe said. "He doesn't get mad like me. I mean yell or cuss. He just kind of looks mean or sad. He told me to give him the wine and he drank some and put it on the seat between his legs."

The police car leading and the pickup truck following were heading toward the reservation.

Suddenly, a few miles out of town, Antonio pressed his foot down on the gas pedal and the truck picked up speed. It seemed that the policeman did not see the truck bearing down on him until it was almost too late.

"Antonio wasn't trying to run into the cop. I thought he was going to, but he was only trying to scare the bastard."

Luis Baca swerved off the road anyway, and there was a cloud of dust as his car skidded into a shallow ditch.

Felipe and Antonio didn't stop. Looking through the rear window, they saw the cop get out of the car. Antonio stopped the pickup truck. He started up again and made a U-turn. Passing by the police car, they saw that the policeman was trying to get his car out of the ditch. The tires kept spinning and throwing gravel.

A few miles down the road, the brothers turned around and headed back toward the police car again.

"Wine makes you do stupid things. Son-of-a-bitch. Sometimes you think about putting your hand between a girl's legs or taking money from somebody or even killing somebody."

They slowed down as they approached the police car. It was slowly coming out of the ditch.

"I drank the wine left in the bottle, and as we passed I threw the bottle against the window of the police car and I made a dirty sign with my hand at the Mexican," Felipe said.

Antonio speeded up the truck. They kept looking back, and soon they saw the police car following them and heard the siren. They turned onto the road that led into the reservation. It was a dirt road, and the truck bounced and jolted as they sped along. The police car turned off the highway and followed them.

Felipe reached behind the seat of the truck and brought out a .30–30 Winchester rifle, which was wrapped in a homemade case of denim from old Levis.

He took the rifle out of the denim case and pulled down the lever so that the chamber was open. There was nothing in there, and he closed the lever and lowered the hammer very carefully as usual. He opened the truck compartment and took out an almost full box of cartridges.

"You remember that .30–30 I used when I went deer hunting last year? The one I let you shoot even though you weren't supposed to before you shot at a deer with it? That one. My father bought it when he was working for the railroad. That one."

They followed the road that led to the village but turned off to another road before they got to the village. The road climbed a hill and led toward Black Mesa, several miles to the south. At the top of the hill, the brothers stopped and looked to see if the police car was still following them. It was at the bottom of the hill and coming up.

The dirt road led through a forest of juniper and piñon. This was near the heart of the reservation. They sped by a scattered herd of sheep tended by a boy who looked at them as they passed by. The sheepdogs barked at them and ran alongside the pickup truck for a while.

"The road is very rough and sometimes sandy, and we couldn't go too fast. No one uses the road except sheepherders and people going for wood with their wagons. We stopped on a small hill to see if Luis Baca was still coming after us. We couldn't see him because of the forest, so I told my brother to shut off the truck engine so I could listen. It was real quiet in the forest like it always is and you can hear things from a long ways away. I could hear the cop car still coming about a half-mile back. I told Antonio to go on."

They passed the windmill that is a mile from Black Mesa. The one road branched there in several directions. The one that led east of Black Mesa into some rough country and canyons was the one they chose.

Antonio slowed the truck and drove slowly until they saw that the policeman could see which road they had taken, and then he speeded up again.

"Aiee, I can see stupidity in a man, sometimes even my own. I can see a man's drunkenness making him do crazy things. But Luis Baca, a very stupid son-of-a-bitch, was more than I could see. He wanted to die. And I, because I was drunken and *muy loco* like a Mexican friend I had from Nogales used to say about me when we would play with the whores in Korea and Tokyo, wanted to make him die. I did not care for anything else except that Luis Baca, who I hated, was going to die."

Directly to the east of Black Mesa is a plain that runs for about two miles in all directions. There is grass on the plain, and there are many prairie dogs. At the edge of the grassy plain is a thin forest of juniper and piñon. A few yards beyond the edge of the forest, there is a deep ravine that is the tail end of a deep and wide canyon that runs from the east toward Black Mesa. The ravine comes to a point almost against one edge of Black Mesa.

There is only a narrow passage, which crumbles away each year with erosion, between the ravine and the abruptly rising slope of the mesa. The road passes this point and goes around the mesa and to a spring called Spider Spring.

The brothers passed through the narrow passage and stopped fifty yards away. Felipe got out with the rifle and bullets, and Antonio parked the pickup truck behind a growth of stunted juniper growing thickly together.

"I took some bullets out of the box and put them into the rifle. Six of them, I think, the kind with soft points. I laid down the rifle for a while and waited for Antonio. He didn't come right away from the truck, and I called to him. We laid down behind a small mound of sand and rocks. The ground was hot from the sun. We could hear the police car coming.

"'Are we just going to scare him so he won't bother us no more?' Antonio asked me.

"I looked at Antonio, and he looked like he used to when we were kids and he used to pretend not to be scared of rattlesnakes.

"'I don't know,' I said. I was going to shoot the cop. I don't know why, but I was going to. Maybe I was kind of scared then.

"When the car came out of the trees, it was not coming very fast. It approached the narrow place and slowed down. I thought Luis Baca would see me, so I slid down until I could barely see over the top of the mound that we were lying behind.

"He had slowed down because of the narrow place, and I thought he would stop and turn back. But he didn't. He shifted into first and came on very slowly. That's when I put my rifle on a flat rock and aimed it. Right at the windshield where the steering wheel is. The sun was shining on the windshield very brightly, and I could not see very well."

Felipe relaxed a bit, took a breath, and opened and closed the lever on the rifle, cocking it.

When he fired, the bullet made a hole right above where the metal and glass were joined by a strip of rubber in front of the steering wheel. It made an irregular pattern in the windshield glass. The shot echoed back and forth in the ravine and was followed by another shot. The bullet made a hole a few inches above and to the right of the first. Another shot followed, and it was wild. It ricocheted off the top of the police car and into some rocks on the mesa slope.

"Three times I shot, and I could see the bullet holes almost in the spots where I wanted them to be. One wasn't, though. But the car didn't stop or go crooked. It kept coming and crossed the narrow place. It stopped then, and Luis Baca got out very slowly. He called something like he was crying. '*Compadre*,' he said. He held up his right hand and reached to us. There was blood on his neck and shoulder."

Felipe settled himself into place and aimed very carefully. Luis Baca tried to unbuckle his pistol belt, but a bullet tore into his belly in that instant. He was knocked back a step and thrown against the car. A last shot whipped his head around violently, and he dropped to the ground. Felipe started to put more bullets into the rifle but decided not to.

The two brothers walked to the car and stood over the still-moving body of Luis Baca. Antonio reached down and slid the police revolver out of the holster, took aim, and pulled the trigger.

Luis Baca, the poor fool, made a feeble gurgle like a sick cat and went to hell.

"They will catch me, I know. There were people who saw us being chased by the cop. Antonio went to Albuquerque and he took the pistol. He will get caught too."

That was what Felipe told me that night when we were sitting at the water tank. He used to tell me all kinds of things because I would listen. I liked those stories he told about the Korean War. That was where he learned to drive a truck, and he had saved up his money so that he could buy a truck after he got out of the Marines. Felipe and I used to go hunting and fishing too.

I sort of believed him about the killing of Luis Baca, the state cop, but not really until a few days later when I heard my mother talking about it with my father. I asked something about it, and they told me to forget it. They said that Felipe would probably die in the electric chair. Every night for quite a while I prayed a rosary or something for Felipe.

Where O Where

November 1974.
Poor Billy, I wonder where he went, where he is.
I know he doesn't have any money. He never has any money.
The only way he can survive is to act crazy and stay locked up,
play dead, or find someone with sense enough to know
he can't take care of himself.
I guess I shouldn't but I worry about Billy.
I take a walk and in a while realize I am looking for Billy Maguirre.
I search a crowded stand of cattails and the shadows of trees
and the saltcedar groves curving along the river.
On the other side of the river are low bluffs of old lava,
and there are many crevices.
Among the bird shrills and within the acres of space between
an owl's hollow and deep sounds, where o where is Billy Maguirre?
Fort Lyons VAH

Sam thought, I should have gone with Billy Maguirre. He wanted me to go with him.

One day Billy had said, "Sam, let's take off into the mountains of New Mexico."

Sam didn't take him seriously. He said, "Yeah, Billy, that's a good idea."

"I mean it," Billy said. "We'll build us a cabin. Not big, just a small cabin with two rooms and a closet to store things in for the winter. And we'll build an outdoor toilet."

Billy was twenty-four but just a kid. He hadn't done very much in his life. He'd gotten drafted into the army, then got screwed up with dope in California, wrecked a stolen jeep in Korea, served time in the stockade. And then he got discharged out of the army with a medical. And then he didn't do anything, like before the army, until he was committed to the VAH.

"I had a time," Billy said, talking about the time he didn't do anything, which had been mostly all his life. "We used to ride in the hills above Blue Valley and shoot rabbits with .22s and cruise our dune buggies. Sometimes we'd have lots of grass. I used to blow lots of grass and eat pills. You ever blow lots of grass and eat pills, Sam?"

"No, Billy," Sam would say. "Not much."

"I didn't do anything. That was the life," Billy would say.

And then sometimes—though just sometimes—with something serious and quiet in his voice, Billy would say, "I want to do something, though. I want to do something. I want to travel, to see the world, Sam. That's what I want to do."

Billy would even get a dreamy tone in his voice.

"Yeah," Sam would say. "See places, meet new people, take a ship. Go places you've never been."

"Disneyland," Billy said. "You ever been to Disneyland, Sam?" he asked a couple of times.

Disneyland. Sometimes that was the kind of mind Billy had. Sam thought, Dumb dreams of Disneyland.

"No, but I've never wanted to go to Disneyland," Sam said the first time.

But the second time he said, "Billy, you asked me that stupid question before. Disneyland is a dumb place to go. Go to the Grand

Canyon, Buenos Aires, Montana, the Nile River. Disneyland is a shitty place to go."

Sam was immediately sorry he said that, because Billy just looked down at the floor. He was quiet for a long time until he said in a very small voice, "I was in Korea once. But that was in the army."

Then he got very quiet again and he looked sad. Sam felt bad for yelling at Billy.

And then lately, Billy got to talking about the mountains in New Mexico and the cabin.

"We can grow things," Billy said. "Radishes. I love radishes. And carrots and sweet peas. And apple trees. I've never planted a tree in my life, but heck, it couldn't be that hard."

Billy was tickled with himself just thinking about growing apple trees in the mountains.

"That sounds like a lot of work, Billy," Sam said, frowning, although he was smiling too. He had come to half-seriously go along with Billy's talk about the mountains. "But it'll be good for us," he said. "Exercise and fresh air from morning till night."

Mostly that's what Billy needed, exercise and fresh air. His skin was the color of old wood lying in a damp corner, and he wandered around looking lost and weary.

Although he wasn't a bad-looking kid, Billy was slouch-shouldered and always wore badly fitting clothes. When you saw him shuffling around the VAH loony, you would know right off there was something wrong with him.

"What's the best kind of wood to use for a cabin, Sam? The kind that Indians use," Billy asked seriously.

Sam was an Indian, but he didn't know what kind of wood Indians used for cabins. In fact, he didn't know much about being

Indian, either, since he'd grown up in Denver. So Sam said, "Probably pine, Billy. Yeah, pine will be okay. Maybe juniper."

Actually Sam liked talking about the cabin and the mountains. One summer after his own time in the army, he tried living by himself in a teepee in southwestern Colorado. Just him and his dog. The next summer he was going to get some land and build a shack on it—nothing fancy, just a one-room shack.

"We better make sure there's water near the cabin," Billy said.

"For sure," Sam said. Near that summer teepee was a small stream, Rio de la Plata, that ran from the mountains nearby. It had the coldest and clearest water Sam could remember from anywhere.

And then, just the other day, something blew in Billy's head. One of the other patients on the ward came running to tell Sam.

The TV set had been on in the rec room. The guys were watching *Bonanza*. A commercial came on. The commercial was a pretty woman demonstrating which kind of laundry soap was best for grimy clothes.

Without any kind of warning, Billy had stood up and thrown a cue ball from the pool table through the TV screen. He started yelling and screaming and throwing a finger at the broken TV, and if someone hadn't grabbed him, Billy would have put his fist through the tube.

Sam watched the muscular aides come and shackle Billy into a leather harness. They smoothly shot him with a syringe of something and took him down the stairs. Sam didn't say anything, and then he turned to stare far away to the bluffs beyond the Arkansas River, beyond the steel-meshed windows.

The next morning when Sam saw Billy stumbling dumbly to the mess hall in a straggly line with the rest of the zombies from the Lock Ward, he thought of what Billy had said months before.

"My old man was really great, Sam. He used to take me and my brother and our little sister to the drive-in root beer place in Grayson. We would get root beer floats. I loved root beer floats. He helped me make an aquarium for a science class in the third grade. I didn't like science in high school but I really liked making that aquarium with my dad.

"He worked in the mines, Sam. That's hard work. Shitty work. Shitty work for this company. Sometimes he would have to work two shifts, but one day he came home early. My mom wasn't home. She was out shopping at a sale. Three times a week she would shop at sales. My old man went to find her. A couple hours later, they came home. My mother was crying and she looked real bad in the face. I don't know what happened. Or maybe I did. My old man didn't say much of anything.

"The next day he moved to Utah. I haven't seen him but two short times since then."

That's what Sam remembered Billy saying.

Sam also remembered watching Billy pace back and forth whenever a commercial with a woman came on TV. It didn't matter what the commercial was, whether it was about a detergent or a compact car or a special kind of shaving lotion.

What seemed to matter was that the woman was very pretty and had this very put-on smile. That's what made the difference. Billy would get all tensed up and his mouth and face would grimace. And Sam would see Billy's Adam's apple bob up and down in tight swallows. A couple of times Billy had yelled and cursed, but that was all.

Coming back from the mess hall after supper, one of the guys said, "Billy Maguirre took off."

Sam wondered, Where the hell could Billy go? He really has no place to go. He has no money. He can't even take care of himself.

A couple of days before, Billy had asked how far away the nearest mountains were.

They were sitting on the grass in front of Unit 8. Sam pointed beyond the hospital and beyond the dike, which held back the Arkansas River when it flooded.

"I was looking at the map in the library the other day," Sam said, "trying to see where the river begins. It begins in the Sawatch Range of the Rocky Mountains. That means if you follow the Arkansas River upstream, you'll eventually get to the mountains. It'll take about six days, Billy."

From where they sat in front of Unit 8, Sam pointed at the river they could not see, his finger following its winding course toward the mountains.

"Sawatch," Billy said. "Sawatch. That's an Indian name, isn't it, Sam?"

Sam watched Billy repeating the name silently. He started to say he didn't know if it was an Indian name or not, but then he said, "Yes it is, Billy."

As he looked toward the river and tried to see it beyond the dike, Sam thought, Billy Maguirre's been gone for half a day now and it'll be dark soon. Yeah, it'll take about six days, maybe more.

Among the cattail stands, shadows of trees, and saltcedar groves, following the course of the river to the mountains, there o there is Billy Maguirre.

Loose

Loose. That's what he said. Nothing else but that. And he repeated it. Loose.

I had asked him his name.

I was sitting in the cafe on Central nursing a coffee. The coffee had gone cold. And he had walked in. Maybe thirty years old, maybe twenty-five.

Brown scarred face, black hair a mess and long. No grin on his face then. A smirk, but a smirk that was not intentional it seemed. Shiny eyes tending toward flat.

That's the way I've been, he said. Years and years. Loose.

He just walked up. Maybe he recognized me. Or thought he did. I don't know. The table was kind of wobbly. When he pulled a chair up to it and leaned on the table, it almost toppled over. But he didn't notice. And he looked at me. Maybe he thought he knew me. I don't know.

Hi, I said. Not loud. Just Hi. And felt I was looking into a mirror and saying it.

He didn't say anything. I grinned foolishly, not knowing what to say next, not knowing what to do next. And then I told him my name.

So what? the look on his face said. So I'm Indian too, I almost said aloud. I thought of offering to buy him a coffee. But he would be indifferent to it. He was loose.

So Loose and I just sat there.

I didn't like what I'd thought about the mirror. So I asked, Where you from?

Denver. Last time, he said. But nowhere really. Here for now.

Brown and scarred. He was looking at me. Studying me like I was studying him. I should have expected that's what he would say. Here, there, nowhere.

Coming from nowhere. Going nowhere. It's scary to think about. I mean, I know what that means. No wonder I'd thought about the mirror.

I've been to Denver, I said. Are you from the north?

He looked away from me. North, south, east, west, up, down. What difference does it make? he said. Does it to you?

Sometimes. Most times, I said. Mainly to convince myself.

Loose stared hard at me with his almost-flat eyes. His voice could have been a club. Tell me then. What the hell difference does it make?

Tension gathered in my neck muscles. I looked down at my cold coffee. I shook my head.

I don't know for sure, I said. But it makes a difference. It's not a philosophical question. . . .

Shit, he said. A goddamn intellectual Indian. What the hell is this? Philosophy. You don't know. You're just another dumb Indian. Just another dumb intellectual Indian. You don't know.

Alright, I don't know.

And alright, I didn't know what to say. But it makes a difference. This was a cafe on Central. It was nighttime, the city's main street was busy with traffic, we were sitting there. We'd come from someplace. And we were going someplace.

So I said, I'm from here in New Mexico. I grew up west of here. I've been other places, but this is where I'm from.

He didn't say a word. I thought, Alright, Loose, you've seen the scars on my face.

And then he said, See that girl? He motioned with his face.

I looked. She was behind the counter. She had a paper cap on her head, and she was busy pouring coffee, taking orders, punching the cash register.

Yeah, I said.

The girl was ordinary—kind of cute, but ordinary. Yeah, I said again.

She looks like someone from Alberta.

So he was from the north. Cree. Chippewa. Probably. He had big hands but he wasn't tall. His hands looked like they'd handled a lot of shit work. Timber. Roughnecking. Brutal work.

You want coffee? I asked. There was change on the table.

He looked at me. Then at the change. He picked it up and walked to the counter.

I watched him wait for her to notice him. The muscles on the side of his face moved. Like in a grin. The girl looked at him blankly and took his order.

When she put the coffee in front of him, I saw her lips move. Asking for the money. He said something again. Her face was startled, embarrassed, and then it froze up. She punched the cash register.

Loose turned and walked back to the table. He spilled some of his coffee.

She *sort* of looks like someone from Alberta. But not much, he said. And then he grinned. Big. And I had to grin too.

In a newspaper supplement recently I read a small item. It was about children in Ecuador who made a makeshift life on the streets of Quito. Running numbers, stealing from tourists. Prostitutes and fools. Indians.

The newspaper supplement said they were a dangerous element—like a bomb—in modern Ecuadoran society. They came to the city because it gathered their energy and gave them a mission. Many of them were orphans. Indians.

I wanted to tell Loose those street kids had the courage to survive. And more than that. The courage would be the redemption of their lives and Ecuador. And of ours.

Loose drank his coffee and stood up.

I didn't ask him where he was going. Okay, I thought. Okay.

Loose, he said. Stay loose.

Okay, I said. You too.

With a foolish sort of grin, he walked away, out the door and up the street.

The Panther Waits

*That people will continue longest in the enjoyment of peace
who timely prepare to vindicate themselves and manifest a
determination to protect themselves whenever they are
wronged.*

—Tecumseh, 1811

Tahlequah was cold in November, and Jay, Billy, and Sam sat
underneath a lustreless sun. They had been drinking all
afternoon. Beer. Wine. Trying not to feel the cold. They were
talking.

Maybe we need another vision, Billy.

Ah shoot, vision. I had one last night and it was pretty bad
awful. Got run over by a train and somebody stole my wife.

He he he. Have another beer.

Maybe though, you know. It might work.

Forget it, Jay, huh? Cold beer vision, that's what I like.

No, Sam. I mean I've been thinking about that old man that
used to be drunk all the time.

Your old man. He he he. He was drunk all the time. He he
he.

Yeah. My old man was just a plain old drunk. I mean Harry
Brown, that old guy that sat out by the courthouse a lot. That one.
He used to have this paper with him.

Harry J. Brown you mean? He was a kook. A real kookie
kook. That one?

Yeah. Well, one time me and my brother Taft before he died in that car wreck down by Sulphur, well, me and him we asked Harry to buy us some beer at Sophie's Grill, you know, and he did. And then he wanted a can and sure, we said, but we had to go down by the bridge before we would give him one. We went down there and sat down by the bushes there and gave him a beer.

Yeah, we used to too. He'd do anything for a beer, old Harry J. Brown. And your brother Taft, he was a hell of a drinker too. He he he.

We sat and drank beer for a while, just sitting, just talking. Talking about fishing or something, getting up once in a while to pee, just bullshitting around. And then we finished all the beer and was wishing we had more but we had no money, and so we said to Harry, Harry, we gotta go now.

Harry was kind of fallen asleep, you know, just laid his head on his shoulder like he did sometimes on the cement courthouse steps. We shook his shoulder.

Uh, uh yeah, Harry said. And then he sort of shook his head and sort of cleared his eyes with his hand, you know, like he was seeing kind of far away. And looking at us almost like we were strangers to him, like he didn't know us, although we'd been together all afternoon.

When we said to Harry that we was leaving, he looked straight up into Taft's eyes and then over to me and then back to Taft. And then he rubbed his old brown hand over his eyes again and said—get this—he said yes, kinda slow in his voice, and careful. Yes, it's true, and it will come true, he said.

I just realized, Harry Brown said slowly but clearly then. Not like later on when you'd hardly understand what he was saying most of the time at the courthouse.

Just realized, he repeated, you're the two. Looking straight into Taft's and my eyes. And then Harry he kind of smiled and made a small laugh and then he shook and started to cry.

Harry, Taft said, you old fool, what the hell you talking about? C'mon, get ahold of yourself. Shape up, old buddy. Taft always liked to talk to old guys. Sometimes nobody else would talk to them. Or they'd make fun of them. Remember? But Taft was always buddies with them.

Yeah, they gave him wine, that wino, Sam giggled. He knew how to hit them up.

Anyway, Harry sat up then. He didn't look at us no more but he said, Sit down, I want to show you something. And then he pulled out this paper.

It was just an old piece of paper, sort of browned and folded, soft looking like he'd carried it a long time. Listen, he said, and then he didn't say anything.

And so we said again, We gotta go soon, Harry.

Wait, wait, he said. You just wait. It's time to be serious and sure. And then in an old-time voice he said, They traveled all over. They went south, west, north, east, all those states now that you learn about in books. Even Florida, even Mississippi, even Missouri. All over they did.

Who did? Taft asked. I was wondering myself.

The two brothers. Look, you can see their marks and their roads. Harry Brown was pointing with his shaky, old, scarred finger. That old man had thick, hard fingers. I've seen him lift a beer cap off the old kind of beer bottle with his thumb. The scar was from when the state police slammed his hand some years ago.

My brother Taft was looking at the paper with a curious look on his face. I mean curious and serious too. I couldn't see anything.

Nothing. I thought maybe there was a faint picture of something, but there didn't seem to be anything. Just paper.

Taft looked over at me then and made a motion with his chin and I looked at the paper again and listened.

They tried to tell all the people. They said, You Indians. They meant all the Indians wherever they went and even us now, I'm sure. You Indians must be together and be one people. You are all together on this land. This is your home and you are all together on this land. This land is your home and you must see yourself as all together. You people, you gotta understand this. There is no other way we're gonna be able to save our land and our people unless we decide to be all together.

The brothers traveled all over. Canada, Ohio, Kentucky, Alabama, Georgia, all those states now on the map. Some places people said to them, We don't want to be together. We're always fighting with those other people. They don't like us and we don't like them. They steal and they're not trustworthy.

But the brothers insisted. We are all different people, they said. That's for sure. But we're all human people, all humankind, all sisters and brothers, and this is all our land. We have to settle with each other. No more fighting, no more arguing, because it is the land and our homes we have to fight for. This is what we have come to convince you about.

The brothers said, We will all have to fight before it's too late. They are coming. They keep coming, and they want to take our land and our people. We have told them we cannot sell our mother earth, we cannot sell the ocean, we cannot sell the air, we cannot give our lives away. We will have to defend these things, and we must do it all together. We must do it, the brothers said. Listen.

Taft just kept looking at the paper and the brown finger of Harry Brown kept moving over the paper. I kept looking too, although I still didn't see anything except the wrinkles and folds of the paper. But what Harry was saying with his serious story voice put something there, I think. When I looked over at Taft again, he was nodding his head again like he understood perfectly what Harry J. Brown was saying.

The two brothers were talking about the Americans coming, and they wanted the Indians to be all together so they could help each other fight them off. So they could save their land and their families and their ways. That's what I remembered a while ago. I thought I'd forgotten, but I don't think I'll ever forget. It's as close to me as you two are.

Harry paused, and then he went on. They were two brothers like you are. One of them, the older, was called Tecumseh. I've heard it means the Panther in Waiting. And the other was one who had old drunk problems like me, but he saved himself and helped his people. Maybe the vision they said he had came from his sickness of drinking—but it happened, and they tried to do something about it. That's what is on here. Look!

Taft and I looked again. But I still couldn't see anything, while Taft said, Yeah, Harry, I see.

And then we had to go. We was supposed to pick up some baling wire from Stokes Hardware Store and take it back to our old man.

Before we left, Harry looked up at us again, straight into our faces. His eyes had cleared, you know, and he said, They were two brothers.

Taft and I talked some about it, and then later on somebody . . . You know Ron and Jimmy, the two brothers from up by Pryor?

Yeah. Jimmy the all-state fullback? Boy was he something! Yeah, I know them.

Yeah. Well, Ron told me old Harry Brown told them that same story too, but they couldn't see nothing on the paper either. They said it was kind of blue, not brownish like I'd seen. I told Taft and he said, Well, those two guys are too dumb and ignorant to see anything if it was right in front of their nose.

Jimmy got a scholarship to college and works for an oil company down in Houston, and Ron, I think he's at the tribal office, desk job and all that, doing pretty good.

I said to Taft, You didn't see anything either. And he looked at me kind of pissed and said, Maybe not, but I know what Harry meant.

Geesus, that Taft could drink. He coulda been something too, but he sure could drink like a hurricane. He he he. Tell us again what happened, Jay.

No, Sam, it was just a car wreck.

Maybe we need another vision, Billy said.

The End of Old Horse

Old Horse just wouldn't let go. He kept chewing at the rope and barking and snarling every once in a while. My little brother Gilly and I laughed at him. Old Horse, he didn't know when to quit.

Finally we got tired of watching him getting at the rope, and we went to tell Tony his dog was going nuts. Tony was nailing a horse stall together for his truck, and he just said Old Horse was a dumb dog.

Gilly said, Hell, Old Horse sure is a stupid dog, hell! He used to like to say cuss words when he was a kid, just like Tony said them. I did too, but I didn't so much as Gilly did even though he was younger than me.

Gilly and I went down to the creek to cool off, and we forgot about Old Horse because we figured he'd quit after a while. Anyway, we didn't expect anything unusual would happen that day. Nothing ever did in the summer. Once in a while there were the Grab Days on the saint's days and that was pretty exciting because you could catch a lot of goodies, but practically nothing else.

Sometimes my father would come home with a funny story. Or a story about something that happened to somebody, but most times we didn't get to hear what really happened because when my father got to telling it good, my mother would say something to change the subject. That's when the story was about something we weren't supposed to hear. Hell, it was probably nothing and we would learn about it anyway, but that was the way my mother was.

Anyway, Gilly and I didn't know something was going to happen that day. Sometimes you never find out about important things until they actually happen, and then it's already too late to do anything about them.

I used to wonder what was the use for important things to happen when it was already too late to do anything about them, like to jump out of the way or to act differently so they wouldn't happen the way they do. And, afterwards, not to think about them so much. But it never worked out like that. And all my mother would do about those important things was to explain them—so that we could understand them, she said.

We were having a good time down at the creek. We were chasing trout upstream into a little trap we had made two days before out of rocks and a piece of curved roofing tin. We had figured to trap the trout in there and feed them in order to fatten them. We caught a couple then, but they had got out somehow. So we tried again this time, but we didn't have any luck.

We were having a good time, though, like I said, and after a while we figured we'd better go home before my father got home from work on the railroad. Gilly had a time washing some mud off his Levis, and I was telling him to hurry when Tony came down the trail to the creek.

Tony wasn't smiling, and my little brother Gilly probably thought he'd kind of say something about the mud on his Levis, get after him or something, although Tony wasn't close family kinfolk or anything.

Tony, like I just said, wasn't smiling or joking as usual. And he just looked at Gilly for a moment. Old Gilly was really scrubbing away at his Levis, and Tony reached down and said it looked pretty good, nobody'd notice. Gilly smiled real big and glad then. And I was about to say goodbye and we'll probably see you tomorrow when Tony said that Old Horse got choked to death.

My little brother Gilly and I just stood there. Silent as hell. We didn't know what to say because of the way Tony said Old Horse was choked to death and nothing after that. Nothing, not a word.

I looked at Tony, but his face was a blank, just like my father sometimes joked with him about: blank as a stoic Indian. And then I looked at Gilly. His eyes were really funny, ready to cry, I knew. But he'd hold it back for a long time, and then when he did start to cry you would hardly notice it. Gilly was like that a lot and it used to bother the hell out of me. Everything was quiet, just the little creek kind of making noise and a couple of birds in the bushes.

And then I said that maybe Tony shouldn't have tied Old Horse up.

That was the wrong thing to say because the next thing that happened was Tony pushed me hard and I fell on my side into some bushes.

I don't know why he did that, push me. That was something, and I was frightened like a little kid. But immediately, or right in the next moment, Tony picked me up by the arm and brushed me off. I was still kind of frightened, and I didn't say anything.

Go on home, Tony said then, and he said he was sorry he pushed me. And then he jumped over the creek and walked west alongside it.

Gilly and I started for home. We didn't pass too close by Tony's house, but every once in a while we'd sort of sneak a look over toward where Tony had tied Old Horse to the clothesline pole. It was getting dark by then and we couldn't see anything.

Gilly was pretty silent, and I knew he was either crying or about to. I tried to take a sneak look, but I knew he'd notice and be angry with me so I stopped looking anymore. But all of a sudden, he said, Shit and hellfire. And spit. And then he started to sob loudly.

I didn't know what to say except to cuss Tony out for being so stupid. Old Horse didn't need to be tied up even if he was a dumb dog. He could have come down to the creek with us or we could have taken him toward Horse Spring to chase rabbits like he liked to do. That was easy. Hell, Tony could have just asked us instead of tying his dog up like that.

I was pretty mad too and maybe about to cry at the same time, so I said to Gilly, Let's race. And I started to run. But he didn't run with me, so I stopped. And I looked at him and said, Come on, let's race. But he wouldn't. He just kept sobbing loudly and hiccuping. And then I said, The hell with you, and started to really run.

I ran hard and ran hard some more until my lungs were hurting more than the other hurt. I stopped and went off to the side of the road and got sick.

After a while my little brother came along. He had stopped crying and he was quiet. I was okay by then too, and I told him I was sorry I had said the hell with him and I didn't mean it. He didn't say anything, but I knew that he believed me.

When we got home, it was already dark. My mother was more or less mad at us. She told us to wash up and come eat supper. My father looked us over, and he seemed about to say something to Gilly about his Levis, but he didn't. Usually he didn't, and he wouldn't tell my mother about it either. Instead he told us about the Rabbit Hunt the Field Chief was having over toward Dahskah in a couple of weeks. Gilly and I were excited about it, and we were all talking about it for a while.

And then my father asked about Tony and what was he doing these days. I didn't say anything, or I thought of saying that Tony was fixing a horse stall for his truck, but I didn't say anything.

And then Gilly said, Tony choked Old Horse to death, hellfire. Immediately, my mother warned him about that kind of language again. And she glanced over at me and then looked at my father. I didn't want to talk about it yet, and my father didn't say anything about it either. I guess he figured, too, that what my little brother Gilly said was the end of everything that happened that day.

To Change Life in a Good Way

Bill and Ida lived in the mobile home park west of Milan. They'd come out with Kerr-McGee when the company first started sinking shafts at Ambrosia Lake in New Mexico. That would be in '58 or '59. He was an electrician's helper and Ida was a housewife, though for a while she worked over at that twenty-four-hour Catch-All Store. But mostly she liked to be around home, the trailer park, and tried to plant a little garden on the little patch of clay land that came with the mobile home.

She missed Oklahoma like Bill did too. He always said they were going to just stay long enough to get a down payment, save enough, for some acreage in eastern Oklahoma around Eufala.

That's what he told Pete, the Laguna man he came to be friends with at Section 17. Pete worked as a lift operator, taking men into and out of the mines. Once in a while they worked the same shift and rode car pool together.

You're lucky you got some land, Pete, Bill would say.

It's not much, but it's some land, Pete would agree.

Pete and Mary, his wife, had a small garden, which they'd plant in the spring. Chili, couple rows of sweet corn, squash, beans—even had lettuce, cucumbers, and radishes, onions. They irrigated from the Rio de San Jose, a small stream that runs through Acoma and Laguna land.

Ida just had the red clay ground that she had planted that first spring with lettuce and radishes and corn, but the only thing that ever really came up was the corn, and it was kind of stunted and wilty looking. She watered the little patch from the little green plastic hose hooked up to the town water system that started running dry about mid-June.

One Saturday, Pete and Mary and Bill and Ida were all shopping at the same time at the Sturgis Food Mart in Milan, and the women became friends too. They all went over to the mobile home park and sat around and drank Pepsis and talked about family. Ida and Bill didn't have any kids, but Mary and Pete had three.

They're at home. Staying out of trouble, I hope, Mary said.

Bill had a younger brother nicknamed Slick. He had a photo of him sitting on the TV stand shelf. Bill was proud of his little brother. He passed the black and white photo to Pete and Mary. Slick was in the army.

In Vietnam, Bill said. I worry about him some but at least he's learnt a trade. He's Spec-4 in Signal. Slick's been kind of wild, so I know about trouble.

Ida took Mary outside to show her her garden. It's kinda hard trying to grow anything here, Ida said. Different from Oklahoma.

I think you need something in it, Ida, to break up the packed clay, Mary said. Maybe some sheep stuff. I'll tell Pete to bring you some.

The next weekend Pete brought some sheep stuff and spread it around the wilty plants in Ida's garden patch. Work it around and into the ground, Pete said, but it'll be till next year that it will get better. He brought another pickup load later on.

Ida and Bill went down to Laguna to the reservation too, and they met Pete and Mary's kids. Ida admired their garden. Slick was visiting on leave from the army and he came with them. He had re-upped, had a brand new Spec-5 patch on his uniform, and he had bought a motorcycle. He was on his way to another tour in Vietnam.

I wish he hadn't done that, Bill said. Folks at home in Oklahoma are worried too. Good thing your boys aren't old enough.

In the yard the kids, including Slick, were playing catch with a softball. Slick wasn't much older than Pete and Mary's oldest. Slick had bright and playful eyes, a handsome boy, and Bill was right to be proud of his kid brother.

I'm gonna make sure that young jackoff goes to college after the damn army, Bill said.

After that, they'd visit each other. Ida would come help Mary with her garden. A couple of times, the kids went to stay with Ida when Bill worked graveyard or swing at the mines because she didn't like to be alone. The kids liked that too, staying in town, or what there was of it at the edge of Milan at the mobile home amidst others sitting on the hard clay ground.

The clay ground by the mobile home had come around to being somewhat more workable with the sheep stuff in it. Ida planted radishes and lettuce and carrots and corn, even tomatoes and chili, and she was so proud of her growing plants that summer.

One afternoon up at Section 17, Bill got a message from the shift foreman to call Ida. The crew was underground replacing wire and he had to take the lift up. He had to call from the pay phone outside the mine office.

Pete held the lift for him. When he came back Bill said, I gotta get my lunch pail and go home.

Is everything alright, Bill? Pete asked. You okay?

Something's happened to Slick, Bill said. The folks called from Claremore.

Hope it's not serious, Pete said.

On the way home after the shift, Pete stopped at Bill and Ida's in Milan. Ida answered the door and showed him in. Bill was sitting on the couch. He had a fifth of Heaven Hill halfway empty.

Pete, Bill said, Slick's gone. No more Slick. Got killed. Stepping on a mine. A goddamned American mine. Isn't that the shits, Pete? Pete. Just look at that kid.

Bill pointed at the photo on the TV stand.

Pete didn't say anything at first, and then he said, Aamoo o dyumuu. And he put his arm around Bill's shaking shoulders.

Bill poured him some Heaven Hill, and Ida told him they were leaving for Claremore the next morning as soon as they could pack their car and the bank opened.

Should get there by evening, she said. And then Pete left.

When Pete got home to Laguna, he told Mary what had happened.

Tomorrow morning on your way to work, drop me off there. I want to see Ida, Mary said.

You can drive me to work and take the truck, Pete said.

That night they sat at the kitchen table with the kids and tied feathers and scraped cedar sticks and closed them in a cornhusk with cotton, beads, pollen, and tobacco. The next morning, Mary and Pete went by the mobile home park. Bill and Ida were loading the last of their luggage into their car.

After greetings and solaces Mary said, We brought you some things. She gave Ida a loaf of Laguna bread. For your lunch, she said. And Ida put it in the ice chest.

Pete took a white corn ear and the cornhusk bundle out of a paper bag he was carrying, and he showed them to Bill.

He said, This is just corn, Bill, Indian corn. The people call it

Kasheshi. Just a dried ear of corn. You can take it with you to Oklahoma or you can keep it here. You can plant it. It's to know that life will keep on, your life will keep on. Just like Slick will be planted again. He'll be like that, like seed planted, like corn seed, the Indian corn. But you and Ida, your life will grow on.

Pete put the corn ear back into the bag, and then he held out the husk bundle.

He said, I guess I don't remember some of what is done, Bill. Indian words, songs for it, what it all is, even how this is made just a certain way, but I know that it is important to do this. You take this too, but you don't keep it. It's just for Slick. For his travel from this life among us to another place of being. You and Ida and Slick are not Indian, but it doesn't make any difference. It's for all of us, this kind of way, with corn and with this, Bill. You take these sticks and feathers and you put them somewhere you think you should, someplace important that you think might be good, maybe to change life in a good way, that you think Slick would be helping us with.

You take it now, Pete said. I know it may not sound easy to do, but don't worry yourself too much. Slick is okay now. He'll be helping us. And you'll be fine too.

Pete put the paper bag in Bill's hand, and they all shook hands and hugged, and Mary drove Pete on to Section 17.

After they left, Bill went inside the mobile trailer home and took the corn ear from the paper bag. He looked at it for a while, thinking. Just corn, just Indian corn, just your life to go on, Ida and you. And then he put the corn by the photo, by Slick on the TV stand. And then he wondered about the husk bundle. He couldn't figure it out.

He couldn't figure it out. He'd grown up in Claremore all his life, Indians living all around him, folks and some schoolteachers said so, Cherokees in the Ozark hills, Creeks over to Muskogee. But Mary and Pete were the first Indians he'd ever known.

Bill held the bundle in his hand, thinking. And then he decided not to take it to Oklahoma and put it in the cupboard. They locked up their mobile home and left.

Bill and Ida returned to Milan a week later.

Most of the kinfolks had been at the funeral, and everything had gone alright. The folks were upset a whole lot, but there wasn't much else to do except comfort them. Some of the folks said that someone had to make the sacrifice for freedom of democracy and all that. And that's what Slick had died of and for.

He's done his duty for America. Look at how much and what past folks had to put up with, living a hard life, fighting off Indians to build homes on new land so we can live the way we are right now. Advanced and safe from the Communist peril like the *Tulsa Tribune* said the other day, Sunday. That's what Slick died for, just like past folks.

That's what a couple of relatives had advised and said, and Bill had tried to say what was bothering him. That the mine Slick had stepped on was American, and that the fact he was in a dangerous place was because he was in an army that was American. And it wasn't the same thing as what they were saying about past folks fighting Indians for democracy, and it didn't seem right somehow.

But nobody really heard him. They just asked him about his job with Kerr-McGee and told him the company had built itself another building in Tulsa. Kerr's gonna screw those folks in New Mexico just like he has folks here being Senator, they said. Ida and Bill visited for a while, comforted his parents for a while, and then they left for Milan.

By the time they got back to their mobile home, Bill knew what he was going to do with the bundle of sticks and feathers. He'd been thinking about it all the way on I-40 from Oklahoma City, running it through his mind—what Slick had died of and for. Well, because of the mine, stepping on the wrong place, being in a dangerous place, but something else. The reason was something else, and though Bill wasn't completely sure about it yet, he felt he was beginning to know. And he knew what he was going to do with the bundle in the cupboard.

The next morning he put the husk bundle in his lunch pail and went to work, reporting to the mine office first. He changed into his work clothes and put on his yellow slicker because they were going down the shaft that morning and he was glad for that for once. He took the paper bag with the bundle out of his pail and put it in his overall pocket.

After they went down on the lift, Bill said he was going to go and check some cable and he made his way to the far end of a drift that had been mined out. He stopped and put the bundle down behind a slab of rock.

Bill didn't know what to do next, and then he thought of what Pete had said. Say something about it.

Well, Bill thought. Slick, you was a good boy—kind of wild, but good. I got this here Indian thing, feathers and sticks, and at home we got the corn by your picture. Pete and Mary said to do this because it's important, even if we're Okies who do this and not Indians. It's for your travel, they said, from here to that place where you are now. And to help us from where you are at now with our life here, and they said to maybe change things in a good way for a good life. And God knows us Okies have always wanted that.

Well, I'm gonna leave this here by this rock, Bill said. Pete said he didn't know exactly all the right Indian things to do anymore, but somehow I believe Indians are more righter than we've ever been led to believe. And now I'm trying too. So you help us now, little brother Slick. We need it. All the help we can get. Even if it's just so much as holding up the roof of this mine the damn company don't put enough timbers and bolts in.

And then he stepped back from the rock where he'd put the bundle and left.

When Bill got home that evening, he told Ida what he had done. She said, Next spring I'm gonna plant that Indian corn. If he's gonna help hold up the roof of Section 17, Slick better be able to help me break up that clay dirt too.

Bill smiled and chuckled at Ida's remark. Nodding his head, he agreed. Yeah, Slick will help.

The San Francisco Indians

The Chief and his Tribe went to the American Indian Center at Mission and 16th. They were looking for an Indian.

They had walked all the way from Haight. A lock hung on the door of the Center. They stood by the door, wondering whether they should go back to Haight, wait around, or call somebody.

"I wonder where all the Indians are?" one of the Tribe said.

"Maybe it's a day off or something," the other Tribe member said.

The Chief pushed against the door of the center again. He searched for a notice, but there was nothing. Just a "Fuck FBIs" graffiti slogan.

"I guess there isn't going to be anybody here," the Chief said. He pulled his blanket tighter to ward off the San Francisco cold.

He motioned to his Tribe, and they began to leave.

"We'll come back later," the Chief said.

Just at that moment, a man walked around the corner of the street. He stopped in front of the plastic sign with American Indian Center written on it.

"Chief Black Bear," one of the Tribe members said. He pointed at the man.

The Chief and the other Tribe member stopped and looked at the man in front of the center.

The Indian man was around seventy years old. His gray suit

jacket was wrinkled and dirty and his shoes were scuffed. He stared at the heavy lock on the door. He carried a grip bag in his hand.

"It's an Indian," the other Tribe member said.

"Yes, it's an Indian," Chief Black Bear said. He straightened his posture and walked toward the Indian.

The Indian man watched him approach.

"Hello," Chief Black Bear said. He offered a handshake.

"Hello," the Indian man said.

The Indian looked at the pavement and then at the young white man with a blanket around his shoulders and beads around his neck. The two others, also young men, stood nearby.

The Chief and his Tribe saw that the Indian looked tired. And looked hungry. And wore wrinkled and soiled clothes.

Chief Black Bear said, "We invite you to our home."

"Thank you," the Indian said. "But first I must know where all the Indians are. Do they come here?" He pointed at the American Indian Center.

"Yes," Chief Black Bear said. "They come here. But the Indian Center is closed today."

"Yes, I see," the Indian man said.

"They live other places in the city," the Chief said.

"Yes," the Indian said.

"Sometimes Indians come to the Haight," the Chief said.

"Yes, Indians are everywhere," the Indian said.

"Come with us to the Haight where we live. Later, when you have eaten and rested, you can come back here," the Chief said.

"I am looking for my grandchild," the Indian man said. "She came to school in Oakland many months ago. She wrote to tell her parents she was at school. Then one day a letter came to them from the school. It said she was not in school anymore. I came to find my grandchild."

Chief Black Bear and his Tribe members listened to the Indian.

"I was told she came to San Francisco," the Indian said. "I was told to go to the Indian Center. I was told this is where the Indians are. That's why I am here."

Saddened by the man's search for his grandchild, Chief Black Bear and his Tribe wanted to comfort him. And they had found an Indian.

"I came to ask the Indians if they know my grandchild. Perhaps they will know where she lives."

"Indians sometimes come to the Haight," Chief Black Bear said. "Maybe they will know. Come with us."

Chief Black Bear and his tiny Tribe and the Indian walked through gray streets busy with traffic. They walked up and down hills. The Indian could not see anything except many buildings and much traffic. And there was a glimpse of the ocean to the west.

Haight Street was crowded. And noisy. And gaudy with color. The Indian saw mostly young people just sitting or just walking. Like the young men with whom he walked, some were dressed in Indian fashion.

Since no one seemed to be doing anything but sitting or walking, the Indian wondered if it was a day off.

Chief Black Bear and his Tribe hailed greetings to people, and greetings were hailed to them. They walked into a two-story building and up some stairs and entered a room.

"You are welcome here," Chief Black Bear said to the Indian. He pointed to a small cot. "You can rest there."

The Indian sat down on the cot and looked around the room. Loud music was coming from somewhere behind the walls. There were muffled noises from the street. The Indian man wondered if he would find his grandchild here.

Chief Black Bear brought him a cheese sandwich and a bottle of wine.

"I'll go see if I can find some Indians," Chief Black Bear said and he left.

After he finished the sandwich, the Indian man lay down on the cot and closed his eyes. He was very tired and drowsy.

He was almost asleep when a girl's voice startled him awake.

It was a girl with blond hair who wore a colorful Indian necklace.

"Hello," the Indian said.

"Hi," she said. "I heard Chief Black Bear found an Indian. Are you the Indian he found?"

"I'm an Indian," the Indian said.

The girl looked at him. She seemed to study him. And then she smiled. "I'm so glad," she said. And then she studied him again.

After a long quiet moment had passed, she said, "We have some peyote from Mexico."

The Indian did not say anything.

"We have songs," she said.

The Indian still did not say anything. But he looked like he was also studying the girl.

"I'm not a member of the Black Bear Tribe. But Chief Black Bear told me that when we have the ceremony, I will join the Tribe," the girl said.

The Indian man saw that the skin of the blonde girl was very white.

"I asked Chief Black Bear to find an Indian to guide us in the ceremony. So it can be real when I join the Tribe."

The Indian man did not know anything about peyote. He had heard some songs and prayers for the ceremony, but he did not know anything about the ceremony. And he did not know how a person could *join* a Tribe.

"I want to join," the girl said. "That's why I'm so happy Chief Black Bear found you."

At that moment, Chief Black Bear returned. "There are no Indians around the Haight today," he said. "I don't know where all the Indians are."

"I think I shall go now," the Indian said. "Thank you for the food and wine."

"Wait," Chief Black Bear said. "We want you to be with us. We have the sacred peyote medicine and songs ready for the ceremony."

"We want you to guide us," the blonde girl said. She reached out to touch the Indian, but he had already started for the door.

"I don't know anything about peyote. I do not know anything about the songs and ceremony. I shall go now," the Indian man said.

"We need a guide," the girl said with a plea in her voice.

"You haven't found your grandchild yet," Chief Black Bear said.

"Chief Black Bear went to look for you, a real Indian," the girl said.

Chief Black Bear and the blonde girl watched helplessly as the Indian walked away.

As he left Chief Black Bear and the blonde girl who wanted to be a member of the Tribe, the Indian heard the girl's anguished cry, "I want it to be real."

You Were Real, the White Radical Said to Me

Geesus, I was about to fall on my ass. Geesus.
Ah man, I get caught into these things. "I'm looking for historical Indians," a woman said on the phone, calling me from a local radio station.

"We need an Indian to be an Indian on our Frontier Days float," another woman had said when I was in a veterans hospital in Colorado.

"Well, there are Indians and there are Indians," the one from the radio station said. "But we need an Indian poet, and you're an Indian poet."

Ah man. And so sometimes I say yeah. And then I almost fall on my ass. Geesus.

I was supposed to be at Glide Church to read poems at 9 PM or so. The California freeway traffic is always incredible. Impossible and incredible but real. So you have to believe it. Nighttime car and truck lights coming madly at you, going the other way. Or passing you, wavering wheels in front of you, the road railing next to you too damn close.

But in San Jose it was good to be at a parent-and-teacher gathering. Indian parents and their children. The white teachers and the school district superintendent looking remote out of bureaucratic necessity perhaps. "Hello, I'm pleased to meet you." They look too bored to be that pleased.

The Indian parents had prepared stew, fry bread, salad and cake. Coffee and punch. I joked with a Tlingit girl who had sung a Buffy St. Marie song. "You have to cook mutton for ten hours like the Pueblos do for it to be really good. And put lots of chili in it." Laughing. And eat it with family and sit around a long time and visit and talk.

A Choctaw man smiled and smiled when I told stories.

"The stories belong to you. Remember. Remember that they come from the source of a community. Community: people and people, people and all life. The songs and words of them come from the nature of all life. The stories come from the source and nature of all life. Remember that." The parents and their children listened to the words, the songs, the stories. The teachers and the superintendent still looked bored.

"You are part of the stories," I said.

A Pueblo woman sat at the school cafeteria table with her two children. "I learned this song by listening to some thoughts about a horse skeleton found high up in the Andes Mountains. The bones were twelve thousand years old." The woman's children were about eight and ten years old. Her daughters.

We swung off the freeway into San Francisco and into the Fillmore and into the Tenderloin and toward Glide.

"We need magic," I said. "We need magic to find a parking space." We found a parking lot behind the church. All the spaces had signs: Reserved. Several spaces were empty. We had no magic. There were empty spaces on Reserve. No magic. We parked anyway.

We trudged up some creaking stairs in what looked, at first, like a deserted building. White rally organizers upstairs sat at a rickety table with posters, leaflets, newsletters, buttons with slogans, cans for money.

At the rally and benefit fund-raiser there were a few Indians. We met Paul leaving. Hey man, I need an Apache brother to talk with, to tell me about the mountains at home. But Paul was in a hurry. Have to go, brother, have to be at the St. Francis in a few minutes. And he clumped down the stairs with a pretty woman on his arm.

There was a large crowd. Mostly whites, some blacks, some Chicanos, a few Asians. A few Indians, but more were coming in. The whites were coming and going. We sat down and watched the people arriving and leaving. It had been a long day and a long frenetic drive from San Jose, and I was tired. I know. I know I feel sorry, perhaps unreasonably, for myself sometimes. I know, man.

Geesus, sometimes. Sometimes I don't know why I say I will do it. This place is a church, man, this is a church. I know churches are places where you bring your tired bones and shredded soul for salvation. But, man. But, man, I don't know why I say yes sometimes.

At the AIM drum, some Chippewas from Minnesota drummed and sang. One of their leaders spoke strongly and eloquently. We are all Indians. We are united. We are all one. We are all Indians.

After he spoke, two young radical whites approached the microphone and haggled with each other for a moment. Eventually, one won over the other, and to the crowd he said, "We need money. We have many expenses to meet. Give what you can."

Coffee cans with handmarked appeals passed through the crowd.

I wondered how Sid was doing in the Indio County jail in southern California. Did he have enough to eat? I wondered how Crow Dog was doing in Lewisburg Prison in Pennsylvania.

Kuntsler, the daddy lawyer of the radicals, his glasses perched at the top of the high slope of his forehead, spoke.

"There is a revolution going on in America. There is a change going on."

He got several spates of applause. And several times he pushed his glasses securely back to the apex of his forehead.

I caught an Indian sitting at the corner of my eye. The red coals of his eyes were smoldering. In Glide Church he tottered from the welling in his stomach.

Several Chicanas and Chicanos in their twenties and thirties got on stage. They sang passionate, rousing songs for the spirited and rising and united forces of The People.

We shall come alive. We are all Indians. The words, music, and stories vibrated. The tense and tired muscles of my body became rhythms.

So it was finally my turn. I thought I was almost ready to leave, but I stayed. I always stay. Even when I am ready to fall on my ass, even when I sometimes feel unreasonably sorry for myself, I stay. So I stumble up the steps to the stage.

Ah man. Ah man, I don't know why, but I do. I do it for myself, for my people, for the source, for the words that are sacred because they come from a community of people and all life. I do it because I ache for help and because we all need help.

And that's the way I read the poems that night. And that's the way I sing the songs that night. And that's the way I tell the stories that night.

The words come from Clay, the old man who carried a brown leather bag on his shoulder when he went from family to family teaching them.

They come from the Felipe brothers who led a New Mexico state cop unto Acoma land and wiped him out.

They come from the brown man with stifled and troubled dreams sprawled at the corner of 5th and Mission.

They come from the frozen and unfortunate winter of Beauty Roanhorse on the reservation road between Klagetoh and Sanders Bar.

Ah man. Ah man, they come from me. They come from them. They come and they come, and I return and return them.

The smoldering in the eyes of that Indian man almost catch full fire.

What Indians Do

Alvin was talking about a play he is thinking of writing. He was describing this one character. "It's this old Eskimo uncle who is listening to one of his nephews," Alvin says. "The nephew is talking about American scientists going out into space, exploring, you know, the unknown depths of space."

Alvin looks around to make sure we're all listening. "And this old uncle says, 'But they don't know that they should look into the space that is in here.'" And Alvin motions with his hands and fingertips onto his chest like the old Eskimo uncle.

Sometimes it's difficult to explain about space inside oneself. It's almost as if it is easier to talk about space that's outside, and away from oneself. Because of that, it's often hard to answer convincingly enough a question such as the one asked by a non-Indian college student.

"What do Indians do at a powwow, anyway," he asked.

John, who is the student's professor, said, "There's dancing and singing and socializing. It's a gathering with spiritual significance. There are formalized dances that only certain dancers participate in, and then are others in which everyone joins. Come and see sometime. Join in. Sing, dance, you'll catch on. It's a sharing."

"Yeah, that's what happens," I said. "It's like a story being told when it's not only being told. The storyteller doesn't just tell about the characters in the story, what they did or said, what happens in the story and so on. The storyteller participates in the story with those who are listening. In the same way, the listeners are taking part in the story. The story includes them in. You see, storytellng is more like an event. The story is not just a story then. It's occurring; it's happening; it's coming into being."

Most people watch parades like they watch the movies. They may wish to join in the parade, but they don't. They watch TV the same way. The world of that box within the plastic box is so far away—removed from their ability to touch or to deal with, in fact. Maybe it's better, though. Maybe it's safer. Maybe it is, but they don't learn much that way. We (they) are too far away.

Some time ago, when my father said in our Acoma Pueblo language, "Yaaka Hanoh naitra guh," I suddenly didn't know what he was talking about. I grew up speaking our native language, and I have heard that announcement countless times. But I've also acquired some formal education in Western cultural philosophy and linguistics and other strange practices, and so for a moment I didn't know what my father was saying.

You see "Yaaka Hanoh naitra guh" literally translates into "Corn People will occur." Or happen, come about, come into being. In a conversational sense, it's an announcement that means "The people of the Corn Clan will be putting on a dancing event." That's what my father said and meant, but what he also meant literally was that the "Corn People will occur." Or happen or come about. Or come into being. Yaaka Hanoh naitra guh. The Corn Hanoh will bring that event into actuality or bring it about. The dancing will be happening. The people will take part in the dancing event. In a metaphorical sense, they will come into being as Corn People in that event. Literally, in a philosophical sense, they will give it life, and by so doing they will give themselves life. They, as Corn People, will come into being.

Because of my Western cultural American education, I was looking into the square world of that box from so far away. I was watching, not participating in the event of my father speaking with me.

I liked Alvin's story about his old Eskimo uncle, and in return I told him this one.

A Laguna Pueblo friend was telling me about his grandpa watching TV one time. The old man didn't understand English very much, and his grandsons—schoolboys—were telling him what was going on within the TV screen. The moon walk was happening. A man was chopping at a large moon boulder with a small pickax. The boys told their grandpa, "Those are Mericano scientist spacemen, Nana. The Mericano government spent three hundred million dollars to go to the moon. They are gathering those rocks to study them. They are looking for knowledge."

The grandpa watched intently for a while, and then he went outside to go to the outhouse. On his return to the house, he picked up a small rock, and then he went back inside. "Grandsons," he said to the boys watching the moon walk on the TV. "I have something in my hand, and I want to show it to you." Their grandpa had his hand clenched together like he held a secret surprise or a trick. The boys said, "Ah, Grandpa, you're just going to trick us," suspicious because Indian grandpas are famous for their trickery when it comes to their grandsons. "No, I'm not going to trick you, Grandsons," their grandpa said. "Okay then, Grandpa, what is it?" the boys said. And then their Nana opened his hand. And the boys

said, "Aww, that's just a rock, Grandpa, you tricked us again!"
"No," their grandpa said with a chuckle, casting a glance at the TV.
"That's knowledge."

Alvin liked that story, and his face looked like he was thinking about that Eskimo uncle looking into the space within himself.

One Sunday morning I got out of bed, and as usual one of the first
things I did was take a look at the *San Francisco Examiner*. I ran
headlong into this headline: PRIVATE PROPERTY WEEK BEGINS
TODAY. And then I had to read on: "The San Francisco Board of
Realtors has decided to tell the truth about Uncle Sam."

I read on because I thought the Board of Realtors would tell
the truth, but it didn't. I thought the *Examiner* would tell about
U.S. corporations building suburbs outside Albuquerque and
Phoenix on Indian lands, taking what little water Indians have left.
I thought it would tell about the Indians pocketed into tiny leftover
enclaves in San Diego County. But, of course, it didn't.

The feature article in the financial section did say that Uncle
Sam "was very much a real person, one Samuel P. Wilson, a Massa-
chusetts meat packer who had a contract for supplying the American Army with beef during the War of 1812."

Yes, it did say that, and it also said that the Board of Realtors
is "distributing copies of the National Association of Realtors' book
Uncle Sam: The Man and the Legend, to all local schools and branch
libraries." They will—I am sure of that—and they will do as good
a job of that as they do of teaching about "private property," but it
will still not be the truth.

One weekend Roxanne and I heard an archaeologist say, "Unfortunately, we have no control over what happens."

The discussion was about interstate highways, Kennecott

Copper, coal mines, power plants, land and water, and Indians. I said, "You know what Indian people wish sometimes? That archaeologists would be really on our side."

The archaeologist, who works for the U.S. Forest Service, said, "Sometimes we coordinate with other federal agencies, like the Bureau of Indian Affairs." They have no control over what happens.

In San Diego, several days later, I was talking about this at a poetry reading, coming down not gently on Americanization. A Choctaw woman who is a good friend asked, "Do you have anything funny to read?" She meant, I think, other emphases and themes in my poetry. She meant that power plants, multinational corporations, and the loss of Indian lands aren't so funny.

Another friend, a Hopi man, asked me, "Do you ever get set upon by Indian people who question what you're teaching in Indian literature? By your writing, I mean." And he explained, "You see, I teach history, and sometimes I get the feeling my people think I'm giving away secrets. You know, Hopi secrets." I understood. The Hopis don't want to lose anything anymore.

So I said, "Yes, I do. That's why I talk about Private Property Week instead," and we laughed. And then I added, "And about the American Bicentennial." With mock disbelief, the Hopi friend said, "You mean it's been two hundred years already?" We laughed again.

Yes. It was two hundred years already, and Private Property Week began that year of 1976 on Easter Sunday. As Charlie, a Navajo brother-friend from Shiprock in the Four Corners area, would say, "Again?!" without any mock disbelief at all.

Roxanne and I went to a Southwest Anthropological Convention to attend a session called "The Anthropologist and the Indian."

Shirley, a Lakota scholar, was to speak on Lakota linguistics, and we wanted to hear her.

When we arrived at the conference room, a white man was speaking. He was an archaeologist from the University of Washington. He was telling about his and the university's efforts to dig up an old Indian village site in Washington. He used the word "recovery." The archaeologist talked about the federal government, the state government, and his own personal efforts to raise money to finance work on the site recovery.

Once in a while the archaeologist mentioned the Makah people, who had lived at the "site" and who presently live at Neah Bay.

He said, "We had the Air National Guard fly the elders of the tribe down to the site." He said the Indians were amazed. When Roxanne and I had walked into the conference room and sat down at the edge of the audience, the archaeologist had looked at us out of the corner of his eye. "Of course, the younger Indians did not see exactly eye to eye with the elders," he said.

We decided to go get something to eat in the hotel dining room. After we had eaten and the waitress had brought our check, we said, "This is a rip-off," and we walked out. The check was too high for a meager tasteless breakfast, and we weren't surreptitious at all as we walked away.

We went back to the conference room, still wanting to hear the Indian linguist speak. A woman was talking. This one was a linguist, and she was also white. She was talking about preservation, and she said there were several universities and organizations who were making the effort, funded by federal and state money, of course. She mentioned a couple of Indian tribes, too, and her wish was that Indian languages be "preserved."

It was getting late in the day, so we told Shirley, who was

going to speak last, that we had to be leaving. "We wanted to hear you, but we have to go now," we said.

"That's okay," she said.

"Good luck, then. You tell them good," we said.

She said, "Okay. Thanks."

The next day we did a session at the convention. We called it "Land, Water, Indians and Power." In the morning I had joked, "You can introduce me to the anthropologists as a wild, gut-eating, savage heathen."

Roxanne laughed and said, "I'll tell them you're a show-and-tell Indian: 'This is an Acoma Indian. He will show and tell.'"

"I'll tell them alright," I said. "And then I'll take it out and show it to them." Laughing—sometimes it's better to laugh.

When it was time for our session to begin, we put up our map of the Southwest, and then I wrote on the blackboard "The Only Good Anthropologist" to remind myself. And to remind them. I didn't show and tell anything bizarre, nor did I talk about federal and state money for "recovery" and "preservation," and when I asked if there were any anthropologists in the session, we were not surprised there were none.

When I was about fourteen years old, I would walk back to the Indian Boarding School on the way from the Sunday movies in downtown Albuquerque, and I would pass by the Sanitary Laundry on Third Street. There was always a continual screech and uneven hum of some sort of machinery in the dim shadows beyond the metal doors.

I don't know why I always stopped and looked into the shadows, but I did. There was some sort of enchantment that absolutely drew me to the entrance to that warehouselike building, but I don't know what it was.

Years later, I was walking up 18th Street from the Indian Center on Valencia in San Francisco. I was passing a building on the street when I heard the screech of a saw.

There was a high, piercing shrill of rapidly moving metal on wood. A burning smell hung in the air, acrid to the nostrils. I reeled through the doorway and saw several men working at wood. Metal tables, machinery, woodburn odor, sawdust, vague light. The din of machinery, saws and drills, the edge of steel, and a bin of pieces of scrap wood. I walked over and chose one.

I remembered the wood sculpture I had made one summer in southern Colorado. White pine, the feel of wood, the smell of the La Plata Mountains, the cool wind. Dreaming, I touched my fingers to the scrap of wood.

"I've worked here for eight years," a man in a canvas apron explained. "You get to do this easily." He zipped a piece of plywood into the saw blade so neatly and quickly that the wood cried against the steel for just a second. So easily and carefully, he cringed with a smile. An older worker with steel-rim glasses falling off his nose glared at me.

I reeled back into the street, the curved piece of wood retrieved from the bin clutched in my hands.

I don't think anybody noticed me hugging that piece of wood as I walked up 18th Street. I don't think anybody noticed the forests in me, the quiet footsteps I have taken in the Rockies and the Smokies. I don't think anybody knew the memory of touch in my hands of the trunks of great firs and pines and spruces.

The smell of sap drove me careening over broken sidewalks, made me so silently angry my thoughts refused to make any sense of that afternoon. The shadows of city buildings lurched into me.

Longing so hard for forests and clean and gentle mountain

wind, I snuck up 18th Street, a memory of white-pine needles cradled in my arms like a baby.

The songs, the stories, the words continue as they always have. Brown children are running around laughing and yelling. An Indian man with a black cowboy hat sits behind an announcer's table. I shook hands with him earlier. He has broad, hard hands, and he smiles big. A Cree who is a university professor says, "He looks Crow. Yeah, that's what he reminds me of, a Crow man announcing an Indian rodeo in Montana."

The man is announcing the events of the Indian Culture Day program at the university. The Culture Day has gathered many people, Indians and non-Indians, from the community in northern California.

A while later, I meet an Acoma Pueblo woman. There is some Acoma pottery sitting on a display table. I ask the woman behind the table if she made the pottery. She shakes her head and points to an older woman sitting in a folding chair.

"Guwaadze," I say, holding out my hand.

The woman shakes my hand, smiling, and says, "I'm fine, and how are you?"

"Fine," I say and introduce myself. She seems to be puzzled about who I am.

Hearing my name, she says, "I guess I don't know you," and then adds, "I still understand the language, but sometimes I don't speak in Acoma." And we smile together.

"Yeah, sometimes I don't either," I say.

When I tell her who my mother and father are, she smiles in recognition and says, "Yes, I think I know who you are now. Your sisters are Linda and Rachel."

"Hah uh," I say. "They're my older sisters."

And then she says, "I guess I'm sort of related to you then."

"You are? Well, I'll be," I say. She explains that her father was related to my mother's first husband, who passed away when my sisters were very young.

"Well, you know, my mother married my father after that. I'm his son, and that's why I'm an Ortiz," I say.

"Yes," she says, "that's true. I've been away from Acoma for thirty years. I go home sometimes, but I've been away for a long time now. I don't know a lot of people anymore."

I tell her that everyone is well at home. She smiles happily and warmly. I tell her I am to speak in a while, read poetry and tell stories, maybe even sing. "Maybe that way you can catch up on the news," I say to her. She smiles some more.

A little girl with sparkling dark eyes keeps looking into my face as I buy a can of grapefruit soda pop from a Chicano student group. I smile and ask her what her name is. She giggles and runs away.

Before I speak, I go to the men's room. There are two little white kids in there. While I am washing my hands, the older one, who is about five years old, keeps lingering at the washbasin, and then he says, "You're an Indian aren't you?"

I say, "Yep, I sure am."

"I thought so," he says. "You know how I know?" The younger boy, about three, keeps tugging at his brother's hand.

I smile and ask how he knows. Proudly, he says, "Because you're wearing red and black. That's an Indian's colors." I look at my checkered shirt and then at the boys and say, "Yessir, you're perfectly right about that." And then they smile and leave.

While I am telling stories and poems and singing a couple songs, there are children running about in the gymnasium. They yell at the top of their voices, and they laugh. I think the words are for them and the voices from all the generations are surrounding them and they become the sounds of running and laughing and shouting.

When I sing about Beauty Roanhorse, I watch the Crow announcer, who looks like an Indian rodeo announcer in Montana, in the front row of chairs. He has a long, angular face and his brown hands are folded together on his solar plexus. He pays thoughtful attention to the song. I think he knows. He knows Beauty Roanhorse from somewhere. From the mountains, from a roadside in Arizona, from some rodeo, some memory.

I know that life is
I know that life is good
I know that life is good
I know that life is good

When the song is finished, the muscles in the Indian man's face are set tensely for a moment, and then he smiles. And I know that the words mean something, that the meaning of the stories, the songs, the words continue. They continue. They continue.

Anything

At the VA hospital when the young vet asked him what he wrote, he said "Anything." He made it sound easy.

That wasn't true. Anything is damn hard to write—that is, anything that is something.

Once he wrote a story about a dog named Old Horse. He had just come home from a trip to the East, and he was tired. And hungover. He had come in at midnight or so from the airport, a bar or two on the way home. His wife was not very happy.

She had gone back to bed as soon as she saw it was him fumbling to lock the door.

The next morning she had said, "There is nothing I can do about you."

As usual, he didn't eat any breakfast. Just black coffee. And he was talking with their son. The boy was three years old, and he had shaken his father awake earlier.

When he had awoken, he was groggy and his head was spinning.

"What do you mean?" he said lamely, knowing exactly what she meant.

"This," she said, her voice an even tone merely stating fact. "You're away so much of the time, and when you come home you're all messed up again. I mean it. There is nothing nobody can do about you. I want you to leave."

Okay, he said to himself. And to her. But he didn't want her to know, so he didn't say anything out loud to her. So I'll leave. I don't know where the hell I'll go, but I'll go. Probably sleep on the floor of the office, that's where.

He had slept there before. It was certainly no home away from home.

In fact, it was a totally crummy place to sleep, right on the main drag of the city, traffic and police sirens all night long, the backdoor night-light of the drugstore next door glaring through the windows. The shadows of the window frames falling on the hardwood floor.

That morning he didn't feel like going to work.

She went to class. She was a student at the university. She took their son to the babysitter.

When his wife and son left, he was taking a shower. He took deep breaths and scrubbed and scrubbed, but he could not get rid of his exhaustion and hangover.

Pouring the rest of the morning coffee, he got this feeling as he watched a mongrel dog crossing the street. The dog was a skinny cur, grayish, a nothing mutt. He felt like the dog. He got this missing feeling for the dog he had had when he was a boy. The dog's name was Bony. It was his brothers' and his. The dog had gotten run over by a damn diesel truck. They buried Bony by the side of US 66, and his little brothers had cried.

So that morning he had sat down and begun to write in a pocket notepad. He used to carry them all the time, all dog-eared and pages falling out. He would jot down scribbles, which many times were undecipherable. He wrote down any sort of thing in the notepads. This time he wrote about Old Horse, a made-up name for the real dog Bony he remembered.

The story, or the beginning words of one—feeling the way he did, hungover and wretched—seemed to be easy enough. But he wrote only a sentence or two before he looked out the window again and thought he might have enough change for a jug of something. He searched through his pockets, and he had enough change. Then he walked up to the grocery mart and got something to make the story come easier.

But the story didn't come easier. Now, as he thought about the young vet asking him the question and his reply, he thought, That's a lie. You can't just write anything and think it's easy. It's not. Nobody can tell me it is. I would tell them they're full of crap.

He thought, That's what I should have told that young vet standing in front of my typewriter who was impressed I was a writer. I should have said you can write anything, but it's got to be something too. But I didn't.

He had eventually written that story—after he had gotten it started that morning—about Old Horse and two boys growing up, and later it was published. But it wasn't easy writing anything. Especially on a morning like that one when his wife had just told him there was nothing anyone could do about him and he better leave. And he had answered, okay, he'd leave, but not aloud. And he didn't know where the hell he was going to go.

A Story of Rios and Juan Jesus

Rios bought a car one day. This was down in San Juan. He used to save his money off Annie and Rita. They worked down on Calle Luna. Sorta dumb but pretty. They were hookers, and they liked Rios.

Jose Rios, soldier of misfortune for sure, he belonged in the loony. He used to say to me, Let's go visit Juan Jesus.

One day, first time I met him sitting outside barracks that used to be a convent, he say, You wanna go visit Juan Jesus?

I don't know who Juan Jesus is.

John Jesus, man, says Rios.

I don't know John Jesus by that name either.

That's him calling. For help or something.

And along with tree frogs and hi-fi going loud in dayroom, some godawful screaming about something.

The world is caving in, Jose Rios say. You wanna go closer to listen to John Jesus?

So we move closer. Under tall palm trees by the hospital. And listen to John Jesus screaming his lungs inside out. Sounds like it comes from the trees, the green coconuts that evening. I think that Rios is gonna tell me Juan Jesus is trapped in the coconuts. The tree frogs, goddamn them, don't even stop chirping away.

I be son of a bitch, say Rios.

So I say this time, Okey dokey.

And we go walk over to the hospital, up some stairs, down hall, more stairs, two, three flights.

Medic mopping hospital hall floor says, Where you guys going, anyway?

Upstairs, Jose Rios tells him.

And PFC medic, that's all he wants to know, I guess. He goes back to mopping.

More stairs, and we listen for Juan Jesus to welcome us or guide us. Or to tell us close up what he is telling the world. But silence. A No Admittance sign on door with little window and wire inside glass. The door doesn't move when Rios push.

Hey Juan Jesus! shout Rios. Goddoggit! Juan Jesus!

Juan Jesus! the hall thunders and echoes. Juan Jesus!

Then somebody begins to moan and cry from somewhere.

That's not Juan Jesus, Rios say softly. And then almost like pleading, Jose Rios say, Shut up, you nut.

And then there's the godawful scream.

Goddammit, Juan Jesus, what you tryna say? Rios shout.

The medics come and curse at us. Get out of here! We'll call the MPs for crissakes! Don't you have any sense? they tell us.

The MPs we don't like. So we begin to leave.

You come back and we'll put you up there with him, the clean medics say confidently and push us down the stairs. Jose Rios, the only guy who wants to hear what Juan Jesus is saying, what Jesus is telling the world, gets push down the stairs.

Anyway, Jose Rios bought a car.

You want to go see the girls? Sisters. I know them. Come on. Have supper and sleep. Come on, Indian, Rios say to me.

I can't, I say.

I heard he never had a car before, don't know what it looks

like, don't know if he can drive, and the traffic is worse than murder in San Juan.

So I say, I got guard duty tonight.

So Rios go by himself. And later I sit under the palm trees and listen and think Juan Jesus is locked up tight in a green coconut.

The next day Rios say to me, You damn Indians, you got some sense.

I smile to see what he means, but he just laugh and don't say nothing. So I suspect and ask around what he means.

What he means was he bust all four tires off his car.

He say, Yeah, goddamm curb.

We laugh.

So one night, late night, Puerto Rican style, calm and damp, little kids all tired from playing baseball in street asleep and dreaming, Annie and Rita on Calle Luna still tricking but tired by now, the MPs or medics or the CO heard Jose Rios yelling up at Juan Jesus.

Hey, Juan Jesus! Goddammit! Shut up! You don't say things like that. They ain't no such thing. Hush up, man!

Along with the screams of Juan Jesus, they heard him.

What you doing, Rios? they ask sternly.

He was telling Juan Jesus not to talk like that.

You better go to bed, Rios, they say. They watch him too, to make sure.

Yessir, he say. But he's listening to Juan Jesus.

Jose Rios listen to Juan Jesus tell the world. But after a while Juan Jesus don't make no more sound.

Rios don't even bother about his car. He just let it sit by the curb.

Don't need a car, he say. He was thinking of what Juan Jesus say. He's afraid. He's pissed off, Rios say. And then quietly Rios say, He shouldn't talk like that.

And that night he was shouting up at Juan Jesus again. Don't say those things. I'm your friend and the Indian is your friend.

The MPs heard him again. And this time, this time with all due consideration and after the medics give him tests, the CO signed the papers and they put Rios up there with Juan Jesus.

Feeling Old

Nome was eighty-one years old now, and he felt old. Felt old. He hadn't before. He had always felt young, at least in his mind if not in body. Of course he did, he'd often thought to himself, even mornings just out of bed.

Then suddenly, in his late seventies, it seemed the muscle all went out of him. And he'd just sit in a chair or on the edge of his bed. And he would even get up painfully and pull the curtains together on his window, then sit back down, and then he'd stay very still in the gray light. But Nome would always get up after several minutes and jerk open the curtains and raise the window to breathe the air from outside.

He'd always done that, never let his spirit flag, never. But that was then. Then. Then during his seventy-ninth year, sometime during, he couldn't tell when it was—it must have happened gradually, subtly—his emotions got tired. It may have been like the redness in his eyes turning to an ache, and he couldn't tell when the moment was that the dull ache began. He just noticed that it was there, the tiredness of his emotion happened like that. He noticed then it was there.

Nome thought he could remember, or perhaps it was that he was trying hard to reconstruct the moment. He'd gotten up that morning, brushed the remaining teeth he still had, felt his beard with his fingers, washed, and gone to the kitchen to put on some coffee. A couple or several years before, a doctor had told him to cut back on coffee. But he hadn't managed to, and he hadn't wanted to. He had said to himself that he'd always enjoyed the morning smell of coffee, and it made him recall years back when he'd rise to go to work at the lumberyard where he'd been foreman.

When the spring mornings were fresh and good, coffee smell was a special tinge to the fresh and good. Back then, years before.

And then it had happened, right after he had finished scrambling eggs in his favorite wood-handled black pan. He noticed the eggs were curdled into a yellow-gray mess. He had put the raisin bread on for toast, and they had popped out of the toaster. He looked at the brown bread momentarily, and then he turned his head back to the eggs.

Suddenly he didn't know if he was hungry or not. Some mornings he wasn't hungry and other mornings he was ravenous. But he always knew one way or the other. This morning he didn't know and he felt uncertain.

The curdled eggs were getting dry, and the toast was getting cold. And the coffee had stopped perking. So Nome sat down at the kitchen table. He felt that tiredness then, and it was in the body and spirit and the emotion.

Eventually he had gotten out of his tiredness and uncertainty and he had worked in his garden. It had been early spring and he wanted to ready the ground for planting at the end of the month. He could do that then, working himself away and out of it. Then. But now he was eighty-one years old.

His granddaughter Alma had come to see him a couple of weeks before. She'd driven in her VW from Baton Rouge, where she went to college, and Nome heard her funny car beep when she drove into the front yard. He didn't get off the couch he was lying on with the unfolded newspaper lying loose in his hand. Alma had knocked and knocked again, and he could hear her call him. Finally, he got up, put on his slippers, and went to the door.

Grand Nome, Grand Nome, Alma said, hollering actually. And he let her hug him. Nome, I decided to come stay with you for a day since you're my favorite fella, she said. And he had managed to smile. She looked around the room and announced, I see you haven't been following your rule.

Nome must have looked perplexed, and she explained. Tidiness and orderliness, Alma said. It was a reference to the years before when he had advised his grandchildren about the conduct of life, how order and neatness were always helpful. Alma started with the dishes in the kitchen sink and moved into the living room by midafternoon, putting the unfolded newspapers into a pile, straightening things, and then vacuuming the floor.

All the while, Alma kept up an enthusiastic chatter. She talked about chemistry, philosophy, and values. Her peers at college didn't seem to know or didn't want to know about hard work and struggle and sharing, she said. And she told Nome that she had spoken about him during a political science class.

I told them, Alma said, that my Grand Nome was a working man from the word go! And he—you!—always spoke for the struggle of the common man! I told them about your years as a merchant seaman and then the lumberyard. They were really interested, and then the professor asked me if you'd come to the college and talk. Would you, Grand Nome? Would you?

Nome didn't know one way or the other. He didn't know. So in order to seem decisive, he eventually said no. No, he said, not strongly or vigorously though, just no. It'll be fun, Nome, come on. You can ride back with me to Baton Rouge. I've got an apartment, Alma said. You can sleep in my bed, and I'll sleep in my bedroll.

But Nome didn't really know, and it bothered him that it was a feeling like he didn't know whether he was hungry or not. So he said no again, this time more definitely. He didn't want her to know that he didn't know or didn't care if he did one thing or the other. He said, I'm fixing my garden soil for planting later this month. He said that to Alma, although he didn't know whether or not he would ever plant again.

When Alma was ready to leave for Baton Rouge the next day, she asked one more time. Nome didn't say anything then. He just sat at the kitchen table and shook his head with a vague smile and then let her hug him goodbye.

Dierdra, his other granddaughter, called him a week later on the telephone in the afternoon. Grandpa, she said, Alma told me she visited and stayed with you, and I thought I'd call you.

Yes, she did, Nome said. It was nice of Alma to visit me. What he said was insincere, but he said it. It was nice of her to visit me.

How are you, Grandpa? Dierdra asked. I'm fine, dear, Nome said. Just fine.

But he was tired and old, and there was no other way to put it, just tired and old. When they finished talking, Nome felt the entire weight of his tiredness and age upon him. He knew that his granddaughters, Alma and Dierdra, meant well, and he could appreciate that, but he didn't think any certain way about it. It didn't seem to make any difference.

Now, with the curtains drawn on the window, the vague light in the room felt like it had the same weight as his tiredness and heavy age.

3 Women

I'm gonna kill him," Rowena said. She wrenched the steering wheel sharply and swerved the pickup truck from the street into the dirt lot by the launderette. "That son-of-a-bitch!" Her teeth ground down on her words.

Annie braced her hand against the dashboard. She didn't say anything.

The truck spun gravel and dust to the side as the tires turned, and they parked abruptly.

"That's the last stupid time he'd gonna do that! The last!" Then Rowena gripped the wheel hard for half a moment, let go, and jumped out of the truck.

Annie closed the truck door on her side and began to get baskets of washing out of the truck bed. "We have so much laundry this time," she said.

Her sister threw her a glare that Annie could feel on her face. She almost dropped the bleach.

Rowena took the heaviest basket of dirty clothes and lunged with its weight against the launderette door, almost knocking over the manager, who was moving to open the door for her. Annie murmured, "Sorry." Rowena didn't even notice.

They went back out to the truck one more time to get two more basket loads, and then they began to stuff empty washers. It was hot and steamy in the launderette. Rowena didn't say anything as she threw Ray's oil- and grease-grimed work clothes into a separate washer. As Annie put the checkered and striped clothes into another, she could see her sister's jaw muscles tensing and untensing.

"There," Annie said with a sigh when all the clothes were in the washers. She was sweating and she could feel the biting odor of Clorox at her nostrils. She knew she would feel nauseated soon, and she would fight it as she always did.

When they finished putting the detergent into the top-loading washers, Annie asked, "Do you want a soda? I'm going to have one. It's so hot in here."

Rowena didn't seem to hear at first, but she finally said, "Yeah, I guess so." And she sank down into a metal chair propped against a dull green painted wall. Annie brought back the cans of soda and handed one to her sister. They sat in silence.

The din was always the same in the launderette. Sloshing water, the change in cycles, wash spin rinse, the whir of the dryers. Tin doors slamming, kids stamping their shoes on the cement floor, Okie and Navajo women talking. Annie could feel the nausea coming on. She sipped on her drink, trying to keep the sick feeling down.

"You know, I married that man because I loved him," Rowena said suddenly. She looked at Annie and then across the room. "I sure as hell did. I don't remember why I loved him, but I did."

Annie nodded. She remembered how proud her sister had been riding around in Ray's car. Sometimes she went with them to the movies or to the store, and she always rode in the back seat.

"We were doing it all the way before we got married. You didn't know that, did you? Because I loved him. The son-of-a-bitch." It was a matter of fact, the way Rowena said it.

Annie didn't know whether it was a real question she was being asked, but when Rowena looked at her she said, "No, I didn't know." Her voice was even smaller than usual.

"It wasn't any great shakes," Rowena said, shrugging her shoulders. "And it wasn't going to make any difference. Because I wanted to get married. Now? It doesn't make any damn difference, because I want to get out!" Her latter words were grim and final.

Not knowing if she should say anything, if there was anything to say, Annie found herself saying, "He loved you too. He told me."

"That bastard couldn't love anybody," Rowena said. And then after a pause she asked, "Did he say that?"

Annie hesitated and then said, "Yes." It was twice he had said so, and she felt uneasy remembering the second time. She wished she hadn't mentioned it and feebly hoped Rowena would not ask for details.

The noise in the launderette seemed to ebb and then immediately rise. Annie tried to think around the knot of nausea in her stomach, and out of the corner of her eye she was relieved to see Rowena staring far away to the other side of the launderette.

Ray had been drinking that weekend and fighting with Rowena. He'd been working on something that was wrong with the truck they had. Annie, who lived nearby with their mother, was watering Rowena's garden as a favor. Rowena had taken the kids to a church youth picnic that afternoon.

Annie knew they had been fighting. She could feel it when they did. She had heard yelling and then the sedan racing away. A half hour later, after lunch, she had started to water the garden. She was almost through when Ray turned away from the truck and spoke to her.

"Your sister is nuts. No offense, but she's nuts," he said.

Annie had to giggle at that. Sometimes she said and felt the same as Ray said about Rowena. But she didn't say anything.

"She wanted me to go to a picnic with her and the kids. And she got mad because I couldn't. Because I have to work on the truck so I can go to work in it tomorrow." Ray wiped his hands on a rag made from an old t-shirt. And he lit a cigarette.

"The boys said you were all going to go," Annie said. Her nephews, who liked to talk with her and she with them, had been excited about the picnic.

"Well, shoot, yeah. I was going to go, but then I couldn't. I can't help it if this old thing needs working on." He slammed his hand on the truck fender.

"I guess they'll be gone all afternoon," Annie said.

"I was going to go," Ray repeated. "But then I couldn't. Rowena said I was just making it up. I told her, 'You take that truck, then, and see how far it'll take you.' She said, 'Yeah, it'll take you as far as the bar, I know that much! It always does.' 'It takes me to work,' I said."

He threw away his cigarette and said, "She started yelling about my drinking. I told her not to yell so much. Shoot, you probably heard her way over at your mother's." He looked at Annie.

"Yes. I heard both of you," she said, feeling a stir in herself for her sister. Rowena had talked, though not a lot, about Ray's drinking. It seemed to be other things besides the drinking, but drinking had some to do with the other things also.

"I drink, sure, but I work steady. And we manage to get things. Sometimes she wants to get things we can't afford, and we get into hassles about that too. Like that color television, you know? I don't even like television that much, but she wanted to get it."

Rowena had been proud of the new console when they first bought it. She brought Annie and their mother over to see it, and she kept putting lemony smelling polish on it, although it didn't seem to need it. Lately, though, Annie noticed that dust was gathering on the console top.

"Hassles," Ray said and shrugged. "But that's married life, I guess. Annie, I love her, but something's not there. I don't even know if it's love anymore. Maybe it's just a used-to-be love. What do you think about that?" And he laughed in the boyish manner he had.

He could tease, and Annie remembered before the marriage she used to laugh at his teasing. They all did. She couldn't help giggling now.

"I don't need used-to-be love, I need some right-now loving," Ray said. Suddenly he took Annie's hand and squeezed it. He was laughing warmly.

For a split second, Annie felt a surge of sensual energy. And then she tried to withdraw her hand. Ray's handhold was strong, and she had to jerk her hand from his. His laughter cut short, and he looked startled.

Annie turned back to watering the rest of the lettuce and carrots.

After she turned off the water and coiled the plastic hose, she walked over to Ray, who was cleaning parts in a can. She told him, "Rowena loves you too, Ray. It's not used-to-be love either. She worries. That's why she gets mad-crazy—like you say."

She had spoken without thinking much about what she said. She didn't know if Rowena loved him. If she had stopped to think, she might not have said it. It was certain, though, that Rowena worried about their sons and herself and Ray.

Ray didn't say anything.

Rowena got up from the metal chair and threw the empty soda can into a trash container with a loud clatter. Annie could see that two of the top-loading washers they had filled were in the rinse cycle. And then she looked at Rowena, who was standing and staring at a woman who had just come into the launderette with a large cardboard box overflowing with clothes.

Rowena kept staring at the woman, who held her gaze down as she found an empty washer right next to them. All the other washers were full. The woman lifted her face and seemed to look frantically around the launderette, but there were no other washers empty.

The woman set her cardboard box down heavily, and Rowena sat back in the metal chair and watched the woman go out the door. After a moment, the woman came back through the launderette door with a bulging pillow sack, and, still keeping her head down, she began to put clothes into the single empty washer.

Annie noticed then the purple puffiness of the woman's white face. The dark swelling was mostly visible around her eyes and on the side of her neck.

Annie sucked in her breath, and Rowena looked sternly at her. Annie said, almost in a whisper, "That woman, her face."

"I saw," Rowena said gruffly, just above her breath.

Without wanting to, trying at the same not to, the sisters watched the woman. She looked totally wearied. Annie felt a shiver in her own bones and muscles. She noticed that some pieces of clothing the woman was stuffing into the washer had dark stains. The woman's upper lip glistened with sweat.

She seemed to be near collapse, and she stumbled as she reached into the cardboard box. Rowena jumped up from the metal chair and walked over to her.

"Let me help you," Rowena said.

The woman had one hand on the edge of the washer. Her knuckles were white. "No, that's alright," she said, stammering. "I'll get it done." And she pushed Rowena's hand away, almost slapping it.

"Okay," Rowena said. She shrugged and started to walk away, but then she turned and said gently, "We'll be finished with these four washers soon." The woman lifted her face an instant and nodded.

Rowena sat down. Not looking at Annie, she said, "She must have a bastard of an old man too."

And then she spoke aloud to herself, saying, "I think I'm gonna get out of it. I know it'll upset Mother, but she doesn't know what I've gone through."

Annie didn't say anything right away, but then she said, "She knows some. And she'll understand." She was trying again to keep the muscles in her stomach from tensing with nausea, but the more she tried the more it wanted to come.

Rowena turned to Annie. Very directly she asked, "Do you understand?"

Feeling defensively small, Annie said, "No, not a lot." She glanced at the woman by the washer.

"To tell you the truth, I don't either," Rowena said. "I told you I love—or did love—Ray, but I want to get out. I'm convinced of that. Being together isn't good anymore. Maybe it hasn't been for a long time. It's not safe or sane for me anymore. Or for the boys. I don't know what he's going to do from one day to the next." Rowena let her voice drift away.

The sisters were silent for several minutes, each in their own minds. Annie's thoughts were mixed with the constant noise of the launderette and her nausea. She wondered, almost aloud, if Rowena had the same sickening feelings. She had to get up and move around. "This one is about to finish," Annie said. A spin light was on.

The woman had been standing by the washer she had filled and started. She looked dazed, as if she did not know where she was. Annie couldn't help it as she said to the woman, "Please, won't you sit down." She pointed to the metal chair she had been sitting in.

The woman's red-tinged eyes locked on Annie's. Annie was about to feel an automatic wish that she hadn't said anything when the woman said, "Yes, I think I will." She took the few steps over to the chair and unsteadily sat down beside Rowena.

The first top-loader finished spinning. Annie brought a wheeled basket over from the corner and began to take the clothes out of the washer. As she pulled handfuls of wet clothes out, Rowena came up beside her and said, "I can't stand it. It's done. I feel like I'm going nuts, and I know I'm not nuts! It's done! That woman just decided for me."

Annie looked at her sister's face and saw she had made a decision. She looked at the woman sitting tired and slumped on the metal chair. Her face was down again and she could see her lips moving. She was talking silently to herself or praying, or it could have been both.

The other washers stopped almost all at the same time, and Rowena started to empty the one nearest the washer the woman had filled. When she finished, she turned to the woman and said, "This one is free now, and I'll be done with this other one real quick." Rowena pointed to the washer with Ray's clothes in it.

The woman turned to Rowena. "Thank you," she said.

Before Rowena turned back to empty the washer, she said, "It'll be alright."

Annie heard Rowena say that, and when she looked at the woman rising from the metal chair and at Rowena, she found a shared faint smile on their faces.

Distance

George had been bought from Macario, a Mexican American farmer who lived five miles south of San Rafael.

"That goat is mean like Macario," the girl's father said, trying to soothe his daughter.

The little girl was crying. She had just been butted and knocked down by George, and her knee was scraped and bleeding. Her father was cleaning her scrape with a clean cloth and a basin of cold water.

"We'll get that old goat tamed down," her father said.

George was a lively two-year-old billy buck. He was boss of the other goats in the goat yard. He stood defiantly in a corner of the goat yard and watched the father and daughter.

The next day, the girl's father roped George and tied him to a sturdy wooden post just out of reach of the water trough. All the other goats, as well as the chickens and a couple of ducks, were able to get water. But George couldn't. It was a hot day.

At first George didn't seem to pay any mind to not having any water. He just ignored the trough. In fact, he seemed to ignore the hard, rough rope around his neck too. He lay down by the post and looked straight ahead. Once in a while, he would turn his head and look around very calmly. It grew hotter by midafternoon.

When late afternoon shadows began to fall longer, the girl's father put water in the trough for the other goats and filled the bowls for the chickens and ducks. George got up on his legs then and for the first time strained against the rope. He looked disdainfully at the post and shook his bearded head, and then he lay back down.

George watched the man for a moment and then ignored him. He lay with his slender legs and hooves drawn up under him.

"We're fixing that Mexican goat good," the girl's father said at supper. The little girl looked out the kitchen window, but she couldn't see the goat.

She had watched George during the day. She felt a twinge of pity for the goat, but her scraped knee still hurt and she remembered the cool water and her father's soothing voice.

The next morning when the girl saw George he was standing on his thin legs. And he was leaning, pulling at the end of the rope tied at the back of his neck. George pawed the ground as if he were trying to pull it like a rug toward him.

Her father let the other goats out of their shed. They drank water from the trough and ate, and then they wandered around looking for shade to lie in. George watched them enviously. He looked over at the man's house but no one was around. It was a very hot day again.

By midafternoon the goat was lying down again. He lay with his head in the narrow strip of shade made by the wooden post. His flanks were sunken and he was breathing rapidly. Once in a while, George raised his head and bleated forlornly, and then he was quiet.

When the little girl saw the goat, she wanted to tell her father that George looked sad and tired. But her father wasn't around just then and that morning he had said, "We'll teach that old goat something alright!"

The next day was the same, and this time by noon George was

plainly in weak shape. His slick brown and gray coat was mussed, the stiff hairs lying every which way like a badly-wired bale of hay. The little girl had come to gather eggs from the chicken house at noon. She watched George looking at her. On shaky legs George bleated, and the sound was pleading.

At their noon meal the girl asked her father, "When are you going to let George loose, Daddy?"

The father looked at his little girl, and he smiled and said, "When George learns, sweetheart, when George learns not to be so mean."

There was a very dry spell that summer, and the hot days that George was tied to the post were burning hot. Little white tufts of clouds started up at the horizon in the mornings, but they never drifted together to even promise rain. The wind blew hotly and even the shades of farm buildings were no haven.

George lay on the ground all the time now, his spine against the sturdy post like he was trying to draw some strength from it.

By the morning of the fifth day, George hardly moved at all. The goat was lying on its side, heaving great, weak breaths infrequently. There were shallow gnaw marks on the dry wooden post. The girl's father checked the rope that held the goat. The strong, hard rope still held George very securely.

The little girl watched her father as he watered and fed the other animals. For several moments she was hopeful he would turn from his duties and take his knife and cut the rope that held George. But her father walked away and began to do something else. He didn't look at George anymore.

When evening came, her father penned up the animals. He checked George and found the goat's eyes clear, not sickly. He even spoke to George. George's eyes stared straight ahead, not giving the slightest flicker of recognition.

On the night of the fifth day, there was a full moon. The girl could see very clearly out of the window of her bedroom because the moonlight was so bright. She could see the white flanks of the hills a mile away. She could see the dark tufts of trees on the hillsides.

She looked toward the goat yard and shed. She could see the post that stood in an open space in the yard. The bright moon made the post white and shiny. At the foot of the post, in the very clear light of the moon, was a shadow. The shadow was very still. And she grew afraid.

The girl crawled deep under her covers, but it was a hot and stifling night. So she threw back the covers and covered her eyes with her hands. But she couldn't sleep. She listened. Except for the crickets, it was a very quiet night.

Then the girl got out of bed and dressed quickly. She didn't put on her shoes, and pebbles on the ground made it painful for her to walk as she made her way hurriedly to George in the goat yard. When George weakly rolled his head and looked at her, the light from the moon slanted into his eyes and made them shine with an odd sorrowful light.

The girl gave a small anguished cry then, and she reached for the knot around the goat's neck. The hard rope was so tightly knotted it was impossible for her to undo. She tried the knot at the post until her fingers bled, but there was no way to undo it. Finally, holding the rope in her hands, she could only whisper, I'm sorry, I'm sorry.

In the morning, the girl's father said, "I'm going to let George go today and see if he behaves any better." His daughter was overjoyed. After helping her mother with the breakfast dishes, she ran to the goat yard.

George was still lying there. He wasn't tied to the post anymore. He was just lying there.

The goat's breathing was trembly and thin and very weak. It was like an empty wind, purposeless and uncertain. The goat's eyes were half shut.

"What's wrong with George? Why won't he get up?" the girl asked her father who was standing nearby, staring at the goat prone on the ground next to the post.

Then, not looking at his daughter, he said lamely, "George will get up when he gets thirsty and hungry." But there wasn't any hope in his voice. A pan of water stood next to George's head. Not moving, the goat just lay there.

The little girl began to cry aloud then. Her father went to her and began to wipe her tears from her face. As he looked into his daughter's eyes, he saw them looking fiercely into his eyes and past him and into a great distance beyond.

Woman Singing

Yessir, pretty good stuff," Willie said. He handed the bottle of Thunderbird to Clyde.

Clyde took a drink. He looked out the window of their wooden shack. Gray and brown Idaho land outside. Snow soon but hope not too soon, Clyde thought.

"Yes," Clyde said, but he didn't like wine.

Willie reached for the bottle and took it from Clyde.

Willie didn't mind drinking anything, Clyde thought. Wine was just another drink, although he knew too that Willie liked whiskey. And he liked beer. It didn't make any difference to Willie.

Clyde wished he had beer.

They had come from the potato fields a few minutes before. It was cold outside at the end of the day. Willie threw some wood into the stove as soon as they came in. He poured kerosene from a mason jar on the wood and threw in a match. After a moment, the kerosene caught the tiny fire and exploded with a muffled sound. Willie jumped back and laughed.

Clyde started to hang up his coat, and then he put it back on when he saw there were only a few pieces of wood in the woodbox beside the stove. He looked over at Willie, but Willie was already taking off his workboots so Clyde went out to get some firewood.

There was singing from the migrant workers' shack next to theirs. Singing, The People singing, Clyde said to himself in his native Indian language. It was a woman singing. It made him think of

Arizona. His homeland. Brown and red and yellow land. Piñon, yucca, his mother's sheep. The sheepdogs around the hogan door at evening. Smoke smell. And good, warm mutton stew and bread. And the smell of juniper mingled with the smell of sheep wool.

Woman singing. His heart and thoughts were lonely. The People singing. There at home in Arizona. And sometimes here and now in Idaho, Clyde thought. For a while he stood and listened, and then he looked over at the shack.

The door was tightly shut, but the walls were thin, just cheap lumber and roofing paper, and the woman's voice was almost clear. Clyde was tempted to approach the shack and listen closer. His loneliness now pressed him, but he would not go closer because it was not the way to do things. The woman was Joe Shorty's wife, and she was the mother of two children.

Clyde gathered up an armload of wood and returned to his own shack.

"Have some more, Son," Willie said. Willie was only a few years older than Clyde but he called him "son" sometimes, and Clyde would call him "father" in return. Willie was married; his wife and two children lived in New Mexico while he worked, like Clyde, in the Idaho potato fields.

"I'll fix us something to eat," Clyde said after he had taken another drink. He began to peel some potatoes. Willie's going to get drunk again, Clyde thought. They had gotten paid, and Willie had been fidgety since they had received their money from Wheeler, the potato boss.

When Wheeler had paid the Indian workers their biweekly wages, he said, "I know some of you are leaving as soon as you get your pay. Well, that's okay with me because there ain't much to do around here until next year. But some of you are staying a while longer. I'm telling those guys who stay they better stay sober. It's getting cold out, and we don't want no frozen Indians." The potato boss laughed, and Willie laughed with him.

Clyde didn't like Wheeler, and he didn't look at him or say anything when he received his pay. He was going to stay on the farm for at least another month. Although he didn't want to, Clyde figured he had to stay since he wasn't sure if he would find a paying job around home right away or even at all. Willie was staying too because he didn't feel like going home just yet—besides, his family needed the money from his job.

"I'm gonna go to town tonight," Willie said to Clyde. "Joe Shorty and his wife are going. You want to go?"

"I don't know. Maybe," Clyde said. He didn't know Joe Shorty well, and he had only said hello to his wife and children.

"Come on," Willie insisted. "We'll go to a show and then to the Elkhorn Bar. Dancing. Singing. All the drunks are gone, so it'll be okay. Come have fun with us."

"Yeah, okay, I might," Clyde said. He still wasn't completely sure about going to town, though.

While they ate a small supper of fried potatoes and Spam, Clyde listened for the woman's singing. He didn't hear it, though, since the fire crackling in the stove was loud and Willie kept talking about going to town. Clyde wanted to hear the singing again.

When Clyde began to wash the supper dishes in the kitchen sink, Willie stopped him by saying, "Let's go. Come on, Son." Willie already had on his coat, and he handed Clyde his jacket to put on.

When they knocked on Joe Shorty's door, a boy opened the door. He looked at Willie and Clyde and then ran back inside.

Joe Shorty came to the door and said, "Okay, just a little while."

Willie and Clyde sat down on the front doorstep. They could hear movement and muffled talk from inside the shack. Clyde thought about the woman singing. He thought about telling Willie, but he felt uncomfortable since he was thinking of another man's wife.

A healing song, Clyde thought, mountains blue, standing tall, strong, clouds above. Woman and song and healing. Women always make songs strong, Clyde thought, almost saying it aloud, almost telling Willie.

Joe Shorty and his wife and their two sons came out of the shack. They all began to walk on the dirt and gravel road toward town. It was five miles away. Sometimes someone was driving into town and they would get a ride. If not, they would walk all the way.

When they had walked for a mile, a pickup truck stopped for them. It was Wheeler.

"Hey, Willie. Going to town, huh? Come on," Wheeler hollered.

Willie and Clyde got in the truck cab alongside Wheeler, and Joe Shorty and his family climbed in the truck bed.

"Gonna have a good time, huh? Drink and raise hell!" Wheeler talked and laughed loudly. He punched Willie with his elbow. He drove pretty fast along the rough road.

Willie giggled, feeling the warmth of the wine he had finished. He wished he had another bottle. Out of the corner of his eye, he searched the truck cab. He wondered if Wheeler might have a drink to offer.

"You Indians are the best damn potato field workers," Wheeler said. "I don't mind giving you a ride in my truck. Place down the road's got a bunch of Mexicans. Had them up at my place years back. They ain't no good. Lazier than any Indian, anytime, them

Mexicans. Couldn't nothing move them once they sit down. But you people . . . for this reason I don't mind giving you a lift into town once in a while. Willie, and your friend there, you do your work when I tell you. That means you're okay for my farm."

Clyde felt the wine move in his belly and its sour aftertaste made him swallow. He turned his head and saw that the woman's scarf had fallen away from her head. She was trying to tie it back on.

"That Joe has a pretty woman," Wheeler said with a grin, looking at Willie. He also glanced at Clyde, but Clyde would not look at him. Willie nodded and smiled.

"You don't get pretty Indian women around the camps," Wheeler said. He turned to look through the rear window and glanced at the rearview mirror. "But she's a pretty one." Wheeler nudged Willie with his elbow again.

"Yes," Willie said and shrank down on his seat. He wished Wheeler would offer him a drink if he had any, but he knew Wheeler probably wouldn't.

As they approached the little town, Wheeler abruptly asked, "Hosteen Clyde, you married?" He didn't look at Clyde, who stared straight ahead.

"No," Clyde said, although he almost had decided not to reply to Wheeler. He added, "Maybe when I get paid more money," and he grinned slightly.

"Someday you'll get a woman. Maybe a pretty one like Joe Shorty's woman. With or without money." Wheeler laughed loudly. He wheeled the pickup truck to a sudden stop by a curb in the center of town.

"Take it easy with the booze," Wheeler said. "Don't overdo it. You'll land in jail or freeze your Indian asses." But his voice held no particular concern for the Indians.

"We're going to the movie show," Willie said. He grinned at Wheeler and winked awkwardly.

"Yeah, yeah, right," Wheeler said with a quick empty laugh.

Wheeler turned to watch Joe Shorty's wife climb out of the back of his truck. He wanted to catch her eye, but she didn't look at him. He watched the Indians walk up the street, the woman and her children following the men. Wheeler thought about all the drunk Indians he had seen in his life. He shrugged his shoulders and turned down the street in the opposite direction.

The movie was about Hank Williams. Clyde remembered who he was. Used to be on the Grand Ole Opry on radio, he thought. Hank Williams sang songs Clyde sometimes remembered.

Clyde thought about the singers back home. The singers of the land, people, the rain, the good things. His uncle on his mother's side was a medicine man. Clyde used to listen to him sing. In the quiet, cold winter evenings, lying on his sheepskin near the fire in the barrel stove, he would listen. And sometimes sing under his breath. Sing with me, Uncle would say, and Clyde would sing, but always under his breath. He had a long ways to go in truly learning the songs, though. He could not sing many songs and could only remember the feeling of them.

Willie laughed at the funny scenes and events in the movie, and he laughed at the drunk Hank Williams. He wished he had a drink again, and he tried to get Joe Shorty to go with him for a bottle. Joe's wife and sons watched the movie and the people in the audience around them intently and quietly. And they watched Willie fidget around in his seat.

At the end of the show, they all walked to a cafe. On the way, Willie ran into a liquor store and bought a pint of whiskey.

"Come on, Son," Willie said to Clyde, motioning for him to

follow. "Help your father drink this Ol' Crow medicine." Joe Shorty went with them into an alley, where they quickly gulped some whiskey.

"Call your woman," Willie said to Joe. The whiskey feel ran through him quickly. He was already in good spirits now. "Give her a drink."

"Emma," Joe Shorty called. The woman was hesitant. She looked up the street first, and then at her children. And then she stepped into the alley. Her husband handed her the flat bottle and she drank. When she gasped and coughed, Willie and Joe Shorty laughed.

Clyde watched the two boys watching them. They stood in the weak overhead glare of a streetlight. Traffic barely moved. A few people who had been at the Hank Williams movie were on the street. The children waited patiently for their parents.

They ate a quick supper of hamburgers and sodas, and when they finished they paid up and walked to the Elkhorn Bar a couple of blocks away. "Do-si-do," Willie said when he heard the music coming from the bar. He sort of danced a little two-step.

Saturday night was always busy at the Elkhorn Bar. But most of the Indian potato pickers were gone now back to Arizona, New Mexico, Utah, and South Dakota. Only several cars and trucks were parked in front. Men and women stood by the front door. Several yards from the bar in a weedy lot, a small fire blazed away, and around it stood a few Indians.

Willie walked over to the fire. Clyde followed him since he didn't want to be left alone. Joe Shorty and his family stood beside the door of the bar and peered inside.

"Here comes some drunks," a voice called from the small circle of Indian men by the fire. There was laughter, but not in derision. Although Clyde at first felt a small tension, he quickly relaxed and began to talk with an acquaintance. With a joking remark, Willie passed him a bottle, and Clyde laughed. After a drink he felt better. Whiskey went into the belly harder than wine or beer, but he felt warmer from it.

The men talked, mostly about The People at home. Clyde felt the earlier thoughts travel into his heart. He longed for home. Even though he had friends here in Idaho, and he had money in his pocket and a job, he didn't belong in Idaho. He was from another place. He was from where his people—The People—lived and belonged. Not here, not in Idaho. Yet some of them, migrant workers like himself, were here, around a fire outside the Elkhorn Bar, and they worked in the potato fields—plowing, cultivating, irrigating, and picking potatoes. Clyde dwelled on his longing, especially when someone began a song. It was the season for sings back in The People's land, and the song was about a moving people.

Clyde decided to enter the bar to get a drink when no one passed a bottle for a while. The previous liquor in him made him sleepy, and he was feeling the cold. He remembered the potato boss's words about frozen Indians, but he knew it was not cold enough to freeze yet. When he entered the Elkhorn Bar, he saw that someone had passed out on the floor. Others stepped over the person without taking much notice.

Clyde met Joe Shorty and his wife Emma, and they all drank some beer together. Joe was getting drunk and talkative, but Emma was drinking quietly. With an indirect gaze, Clyde watched the woman's face as he tried to remember the song. But he could not— it was too noisy in the Elkhorn Bar. He looked at the eight- and ten-year-old Shorty boys standing by the jukebox, staring at the disks spinning around and around.

He went to look for Willie. When Clyde found him, Willie

said, "So there you are, my son." His voice was slurred with booze. He was drunk, and he handed Clyde a nearly empty bottle. "Welcome home, welcome home," Willie said with a maudlin, quavery laugh.

Now very few in number, the Indians at the fire were singing in the high voice of The People. Like the wind flowing through clefts in the mountains. Clyde wondered if it was the booze that made him hear the wind in the singing. But no, he decided, it *was* the wind in the mountains. And yes, he knew, it *was* The People's men who sang the songs. And yes, he also knew, it *was* also the drunken men of The People who sang the songs.

Clyde drank some more, but he was getting tired and colder. He told Willie he wanted to go back to the camp.

"No, my son, you must stay," Willie said. "It is a long night yet. The ceremony nights are long. The singing will last all night long. You must stay until it is finished." Although inebriated, Willie spoke in their native language now. His words had a deliberate and lasting presence they did not have in the broken English he spoke other times.

Clyde wanted to tell Willie this Idaho potato land was not The People's home. He wanted to tell the other Indian men that. But outside of the Elkhorn Bar, standing around a weak little fire, he knew they would not pay attention to him. Clyde remembered: *The fire would be big, and when it grew smaller someone would bring armloads of wood and throw the wood on the fire. Their children would wander through the crowd.* Here, the only children were the boys by the jukebox who watched the spinning records. *In the mornings, there were newly built roaring fires before family camps, and the mountains of The People upon which dawnlight fell showed there would be falling snow soon.* Here by the Elkhorn Bar there would be only the ashes of a cold, dead fire, and no one would see the coming light in the east. Maybe, like Wheeler said, there will be frozen-ass Indians lying around.

Clyde walked away from the fire, the singing Indians, and the Elkhorn Bar. The town was quiet. A police cruiser drove in the direction of the bar, and the officer behind the wheel looked at Clyde, but the cruiser didn't stop. When he got to the edge of town, Clyde lengthened his stride.

When he had walked for a while, he realized that someone was walking ahead of him. Soon he recognized it was Emma and her two children. Joe Shorty's family—but Joe was not with them. Joe Shorty must have stayed at the bar, Clyde thought, and his family had left without him. Clyde slowed his walking by shortening his stride. He felt uncomfortable since Emma and her sons were Joe Shorty's family. But the boys heard the fall of his footsteps on the road behind them. Loudly one of them said, "It's Clyde Hostiin! Clyde, Clyde come walk with us!" The woman and the boys stopped and let Clyde catch up to them.

The woman was slightly drunk. In the dark under a night sky with only a few stars shining, Clyde could see her smile. She staggered some. "We left Joe Shorty at the bar. He's going to come home in the morning."

The woman and her sons and Clyde walked quietly and steadily. Clyde looked back once, and he could barely make out a pale light over the town. The late night was cold but not windy, and Clyde lifted his hands out of his pockets to test the cold. Willie will be alright, Clyde thought. He and Joe Shorty will come back together to the camp in the morning.

Suddenly, the lights of a vehicle lit them up from behind. Clyde said, "We better move to the side of the road." The younger boy stumbled in the dark and grabbed ahold of Clyde's hand. The boy's hand was cold, and Clyde felt slightly awkward with Joe Shorty's son's hand in his.

Clyde instantly recognized that the vehicle was Wheeler's pickup truck. It passed them in a cloud of dust, then slowed to a stop fifty yards ahead. Wheeler honked the horn. Clyde and Joe Shorty's family walked toward the truck as it backed up.

"It is Wheeler. The potato boss," Clyde said to the woman. She did not look at him or say anything. The younger son clung to his mother's skirt.

The pickup truck stopped as they reached it. Wheeler rolled down his window and studied them for a moment. Wheeler looked at Clyde and winked. Clyde felt a small panic rise in him when he realized the younger child's hand was still in his. "Well, come on. Get in," Wheeler said. And then he climbed out of his truck, unzipped his fly, and urinated by the side of the road next to his truck.

Emma and her children and Clyde climbed into the back of the truck. When Wheeler saw they had all climbed in back, he said gruffly, "Come on, get in front." And then in a softer tone, he said, "There's enough room in front, and it's damn cold out." Wheeler held his hand out to the boys, but they hung back. He grabbed the younger boy and swung him over the side of the truck. Emma and her older son had no choice but to follow.

Clyde's feelings emptied suddenly, swiftly, but for only a moment, and then he felt himself burning. He watched Emma climb out of the back of the truck and into the cab. When he jumped down from the back and got into the front, he felt light and springy. He purposely grinned at Wheeler.

Emma was quiet. Sitting very still on the truck seat, she stared straight ahead at the dashboard.

"Joe Shorty must be having a good time at the Elkhorn Bar,"

Wheeler said loudly. He steered wildly to keep the truck on the bumpy dirt road.

The woman held her younger son on her lap and the older one huddled tightly against her side. Clyde was braced against the door. He could feel Emma's movement and her warmth. He looked straight ahead at the road lit up by the truck lights.

"Hosteen Clyde. Weren't you having a good time?" Wheeler spoke directly to him, more than just the hint of an edge in his voice. "Maybe there's a good time some other place, huh?"

Clyde felt hot liquid surge in him. It was very warm in the truck, almost hot, and the heater fan was blowing on his ankles. It's the whiskey, Clyde said to himself. What does this man Wheeler think of this? And then he thought of what all the white men in the world thought about all the Indians in the world. I'm drunk, Clyde thought. Too much whiskey and wine. I'm drunk. He wanted to sing that in his own language, The People's language, but there didn't seem to be any right words for it. It was awkward and odd, somehow, to come up with words for that in his own language. And when he as an Indian thought about it in English and in song, it was silly and absurd and pointless.

Clyde grinned again at Wheeler directly, but Wheeler wasn't paying attention to him now.

Wheeler drove the truck with one hand and with the other he patted Joe Shorty's son on the head, and he smiled at Joe Shorty's wife.

"Nice kid. Nice kid," Wheeler said. Emma moved nervously, warily, and she clutched her sons tightly to her.

Clyde felt Emma move, and he was tense because of her nervous energy. He tried to think of the song he had heard her singing. The People singing, he thought. Yes, the woman singing. The mountains, the living land, the women strong, the men strong, the children strong. But Clyde was tense, and he had to take deep, slow breaths until finally he said, silently, Okay, potato boss, okay.

Wheeler drove his truck into the potato field workers' camp and stopped in front of Clyde's and Willie's shack. Clyde again thought, Okay, potato boss, okay. He opened the door and began to get out of the truck. Emma and her children began to follow him.

"I'll drive you home," Wheeler said. The tone of his voice was calm and low key but firm and almost commanding. And then in a softer voice, and faintly smiling, he said, "I'm going your way."

And then Wheeler put his hand on Emma's arm, but she wrenched her arm away from him. Clyde stopped and looked at Wheeler.

Wheeler scowled and spoke under his breath. And then he reached underneath the truck seat for a paper bag with a bottle, which he put on the seat beside him. Emma did not move away anymore. She looked at Wheeler's face for a moment, although avoiding his eyes. And then with a soft voice she spoke briefly in Indian to her sons. Clyde heard her too, and he could not help but be shocked speechless by what she said. With his thoughts on his face, he looked at her and wished she would turn her eyes toward him. *The song, the song. Woman singing.* Clyde tried very hard to think of the song he had heard her singing. The children jumped out of the truck then and ran home to their migrant worker's shack. Emma and the potato boss Wheeler followed.

Clyde stood behind the door of his and Willie's shack for a long time, listening to and feeling his angry and painful thoughts. He thought of Willie, Joe Shorty, the Elkhorn Bar, Hank Williams, Idaho, potato fields, Emma, her sons, Arizona, home. And he thought of the potato boss Wheeler and himself. And Emma again. But not the song, and not the woman singing the song. Clyde asked himself why he was not listening for the song anymore. And he told himself it was because he had decided that the woman singing was something a long time ago. It was something from another time and another place, and it would not happen again. If it did, Clyde would not believe it. He would not listen. And he would not hear.

Finally, he moved away from the door. Then he began to search through Willie's things for a bottle of something. But there was no bottle of anything, except the mason jar of kerosene. For a moment, Clyde thought of drinking the kerosene, but it was a silly and crazy thought and he laughed.

In the morning when the bus was pulling out of town, Clyde thought of Willie again. Red-eyed and sick, Willie had come in when the sun was rising. "We had a good time, Son," Willie had said. He had sat down at the table woodenly.

Willie did not notice that Clyde was putting his clothes into a grip bag. "That Wheeler, he sure gets up early. Joe Shorty and I met him outside his house. 'The early bird gets the worm,' he said. Sure a funny guy. He gave us some drinks." Barely coherent, Willie mumbled. He was about to fall asleep with his head on the table.

"I'm going home, Father," Clyde said. He had finished putting his clothes into the bag. By then Willie was passing out, and he didn't hear what Clyde said.

When Clyde thought about the woman's singing, he knew it had been real. Later on, when he heard the singing again somewhere, he knew that he would believe it. Now as the bus was leaving, he began to sing the song he had heard the woman singing. Even though there was a knotted ache in his throat, he began to sing the feeling of the woman singing.

Crossing

After five years in California, Charley Colorado was on his way back home to New Mexico. He had stopped to visit with his sister Dianne, who lived in Palo Alto.

"Five years," Charley said. "I don't know what I expected, but I don't have much to show for having come to California."

It was late afternoon, and they had been talking for a long time in Dianne's apartment. It was different now; that much was certain. Dianne was finishing law school, and Charley had worked in San Francisco for the past several years. Indians were in places they had never been. They were doing things they had never done. Charley and Dianne had talked about that, and now they had grown quiet.

After a while, Charley picked up a framed photograph from a TV stand. He turned it over and read: Charles and Dianne, 1961.

"I didn't know you had this," Charley said. "Do you remember where the photo was taken?"

"It was in southern California where Dad was working. Mama, you, and I went to visit him that summer. You were in your first year of Indian Boarding School," Dianne said.

"We went by train," Charley said. "Dad met us in Barstow, and we stayed with relatives at the Indian colony. The next day, we went where the track gang was, near San Clemente. You and I wanted to see the ocean right away. We all walked down to the beach. I was so excited and scared when the ocean came into view. Seeing it took my breath away."

"You look so serious in the picture, Charley," Dianne said with a small laugh. "Just like you look now."

Charley laughed too. "I was scared. I didn't like where Dad was living. That bunk boxcar. The whole thing would shake whenever a train passed by on the next track."

"We didn't stay there long," Dianne said. "We went back to Barstow to the Indian colony. Such a name, but that's what it was. The railroad company brought Indian people as workers from New Mexico and put them in little firetrap houses on company-owned land by the railroad yards."

The brother and sister both knew very certainly what had happened. After the AT&SF RY had taken the very best farming lands for its route along the river in the 1890s, Indians couldn't make a living from the land they had left. So in meager compensation they had taken jobs laboring for the railroad.

"Daddy would come home from laying and repairing track, and he would be all dirty and exhausted, groaning from pained muscles. It's no wonder he and other men drank until they couldn't feel anything."

Charley would be dismayed. His father's speech would become slurred. He would stagger and stumble around when usually he was so graceful. Drunkenness was common at the Indian colony. There were always fights; there was always screaming and yelling. Charley would hide every time his father got drunk. At the Indian colony he would see the men trudging off to work in the morning and returning in the evening looking like they had just lost a battle.

"Do you remember that story Grandpa Santiago would tell?" Dianne said. "It was after the railroad came, I think. Things were so poor. The people were sick. There wasn't much to eat. There was little useful farming land left. The men decided to leave the Pueblo to find work." Dianne was simply stating a fact and a remembrance told by their grandfather when they were children.

"He said, 'The men packed provisions for a long journey on burros and horses. Some men had neither, so they were to take turns riding and walking. I was this tall, just a little boy. There was a great flurry of activity and excitement—and apprehension, for who knew what might happen. Events were unforeseen, and there were dangers. But being very young, I found it of great excitement. There was much sadness and weeping, though, upon the leave-taking. Mothers, grandmothers, wives, daughters, sisters, sons, beloved ones were all crying and calling out to the men. Be well, avoid danger, have courage on your journey, return to us safely. May fortune and the guiding spirits of our people be with you. We love you.

"'As the men left, they sang this song:

Kalrrahuuriniah tse
Kalrrahuuriniah tse
Steh ehyuu uuh.

"'From the edge of our Pueblo, our homeland, we watched them until they disappeared into the west.'"

Yes, Charley remembered clearly his grandfather speaking when he told that story. His voice had been somewhat sad but always resolute with the knowledge of what the people had to do.

"'There was an old, old woman who could not see very well, who kept looking toward the west long after the men had left. She kept murmuring prayers and saying: *Tell the rain to come, young men. When you meet the Shiwana at the western edge, tell them we need their help. Bring the rain home with you, young men, from the great water. Your journey will be for all of us and for the land, young men.* And she sang. My brother and I stood with the old woman until it was too dark to see anything but the faint light over the western mountains and a few red clouds, which I imagined were dust clouds raised by the men and their horses and burros.'"

"The people from the Pueblo decided to do what was necessary," Dianne said. "There was nothing else they could do. It may sound kind of odd, but they were like the Okies who, later on, came to California too. What land they had left was worthless. No living could be made from it. The people were forced off the land."

Charley had asked his mother for details of the journey taken by the men. She said: They arrived at a big river after they had traveled for many days. At the river they were stopped by Mericano white men who demanded payment for crossing the river. The men had guns, and they told our beloved ones they could cross only if they made payment for passage on a boat.

The men didn't have any money. All they had was their desire to work. That's why they had made the decision to go to California. So they didn't know what to do at first. Some wanted to cross at another location, but others said it would be dangerous. There were men on the other side of the river who would demand paper evidence of having paid for crossing the river. Some men said it was fruitless to go on and they wanted to turn back and go home.

At that point, the elder leaders said, "We have to be of one mind and purpose, and we all have to decide what to do. We came on this journey to find work because we have the ability and desire to work. But it is obvious these Mericano-titra here will not let us pass without payment of money to them, and they have said they do not want more Indians in their state anyway. We have a purpose and it's to help our people who are suffering a difficult time. We must remember them."

So the men beloved, Charley's mother had said, decided to sell what possessions they had, their burros and horses, even their weapons, in order to pay for the passage of several of their number. It was a sad time. When the men who couldn't cross the river returned home, they had almost nothing left. It was about 1911, a dim and hard time for our people then.

Dianne said, "For a long time, I thought the story was kind of sad because most of the men didn't get to Kalrrahuuriniah tse and returned home with nothing. But then, thinking about it, it's not sad. The men decided what to do. They sold everything in order for a few of them to go on. They didn't just turn back. A few would make that crossing for whatever it meant. To make a living, to summon the rain from the ocean. Just like they had all set out to do. I only heard Grandpa Santiago tell the story when we were children but I remember every detail."

The next morning came with the sunlight streaming through thin curtains onto the red carpet of Dianne's apartment. For several moments, Charley, lying face down on the edge of a sofa bed, could not shake the dream that was happening. First One was shouting, "Come, hurry, we're almost there!"

He could barely hear his brother's shout as it came from a vast distance across a valley filled with a river of molten volcanic lava that hissed and sputtered and leaped up in rippling surges. Like his brother, who had already done so, Second One was to cross the valley of fiery lava.

But Second One was afraid, and he was trembling. First One called to him again. Even at a distance, Second One could see that where his brother was the land was green and lush with grass, plants, and trees. And above the trees and in the sky beyond were clouds, white and dark thunderclouds.

The brothers had been sent to take word to the Shiwana, the rain clouds. But Second One's fear froze him to the ground, and he could not move. The very ground he stood upon was rocky and barren and shook with the powerful surging of the molten rock. Second One was desperate. He did not want to fail. The people and the land were waiting for rain.

Then faintly, very faintly, across the vast, fearsome valley, he heard First One's voice: "Look behind you!"

Second One looked. There was nothing but barren, rocky hills and dried tree trunks and beyond that the flat white sky. What was he to see? Second One moaned with a dry, parched throat. And then in the distance, indistinct at first, he saw there was someone coming very slowly. His eyes burning painfully, Second One strained to see who it was.

It was an old woman with white hair. Slowly and painfully, she was making her way among huge boulders in her way. She was feeling the huge boulders with her hands, making her way slowly. She could not see. She was blind! Without thinking, Second One ran to her and said, "Grandmother, there is danger ahead. You must not walk toward it. Turn back! Turn back!" The old woman looked at him with her white-turned eyes and said, "Grandson, I have come to help you on your mission to help the people and the land."

She was so old even her words were slow. She put her hand in her apron pocket and brought out a flowered handkerchief that was knotted. Untying the knot, she showed Second One a white stone nestled in cornmeal. With her fingers, the old woman picked up the stone and handed it to Second One.

"Take this, Grandson. Tie it to your arrow and let your arrow fly across to the other side of the valley." The old woman took the cornmeal in her hand and breathing upon it all around in a circle to the horizons, she sprinkled it on the ground and shook out her handkerchief.

Second One did as he was told. He quickly tied the stone to the arrow shaft with sinew. He put the arrow to his bow and then pulled the bowstring with all his might, and he let the arrow fly! It flew and flew until Second One lost sight of it. Then in the path of its flight there appeared a silver thread shining and arcing above the ferocious valley of fiery lava!

"Quickly, Grandson," the old woman said. "Climb on the shining road. Go as fast as you can run."

And so calling, "Thank you, Grandmother!" Second One climbed on the silver thread and ran as fast as he could to the other side of the valley. From below, he could feel the furious red heat of the lava leaping up at him.

Charley shook his head and squinted his eyes at the morning light falling on his face and the red carpet. "Thank you," he said quietly. "All around and beyond, thank you for the journey here and for the journey home to the Pueblo. Thank you."

Hiding, West of Here

I got to thinking of it all.

This mountain has been here for a long, long time. Just being here, sitting and sprawling and rising tall, growing trees, grass, oak brush. Boulders and slab rock slowly sliding down the sides of the mountain.

Funny, I never thought about it before. I mean, I come up here a lot, and I've seen it and I've felt it. Usually I come up that road from Grants into Lobo Canyon, following the little creek running by the road, then up this way. And I drive off the road a ways on a little dirt road that nobody ever uses much and I sort of hide.

Yeh, sort of hide you might call it, my car off in the trees.

I guess even thinking I'd park the car so nobody could see it if they happen to be passing by on the bigger road. And then I come sit on some rocks, like this one here.

Well, that's what makes me think about it now, sitting here by the mountain, on the mountain, that peak behind me, rocks around me.

Because one afternoon I was sitting here, sort of hidden, and . . . well, I'll explain it.

I work on the other side of that long lava mesa at Ambrosia Lake at a mine section there. I come out from home, West Virginia, in 1958, got on at Kerr-McGee, then quit and went over to Phillips for a while. And then back to Kerr-McGee again until I quit for a while. But I got a trade as a mechanic, and the pay's good, and I don't have to go underground much anymore. I'm back with the company again. I had to work shift before, but now it's all days, five days a week. Kids out of high school and all grown. My youngest daughter in nursing school. So I'm doing alright.

But being a mechanic at the mines, it's still hard work. Cold in winter, hotter'n the dickens in the summer. Even underground, when the ventilation goes out, you have to go down and get it back in operation—that's the shits. And new guys coming on all the time, you can't depend on them. Some bums come to work shaky and badminded, give everyone trouble, can't trust them with tools and equipment. Accidents. I've seen some bad ones. Company's fault, most of them, but it don't ever look that way. Superintendent, company rules and regulations set up that way; a man can't do anything to make him feel ahead.

I've worked hard all my life. My daddy was a coal miner. Grandpa too. It's work that's hard. Sometimes you feel good and strong, but it's shitwork too, so you feel there's no profit in being a man. So I come sometimes on Sundays, come up here, and well, yeah, hide out. It's my time, the mountain at my back, over my shoulder. And I can't hear anything except the wind brushing through the trees and laying onto the cliffs. These here, at my feet. It's my time and the mountain's time.

One afternoon I was here just kind of listening, watching sparrows or some kind of bird a while. And then I heard some breathing hard. I mean man kind of breathing, heavy and low on breath, like some fellow down in the mine shoveling rock ore. Or drilling, and he's not used to it. I used to wonder why anybody would torture themselves like that, but they got to make a living. Well, I heard that breathing, and I looked around, but I couldn't see anything and then I figured it to be coming from below. And I looked down there, past the cliff edge, and I seen these Indians, two of them.

They were coming uphill, coming out of the trees, pines, coming toward the bottom of the cliff, and they were puffing away, the old man mostly. He was pretty old, late eighties, maybe ninety. And a younger man about fifty, who looked older than he actually was due to a heavy gut and a tired face. Sweat was pouring off him. The old man was actually in pretty good shape but for his breathing like I've known guys breathe at home with the black lung. They can't breathe, and they can't climb mountains. Not like this old guy.

Well, those Indians, they were up to something, I could tell that. They were dressed in blankets wrapped around them. I mean, colored blankets were wrapped around their hips and shoulders, and they had beads around their necks and a little pouch at their sides. I seen pictures of Indians about like that.

I've worked with several younger Indian fellows about twenty and thirty years old. One of the younger ones once, I asked him why he wore a little bag on his leather belt. He was the only one who did. We were eating lunch, and he looked up at me, and he drank some coffee from his thermos cup, and then he said, You know that stope we was working this morning? And I said yeah. Well, he said, you know that ain't very well shored and you notice some bolts cracking loose. I'd noticed them, and I said yeah. He patted his pouch and he said, Well, this keeps it from falling down on us 'cause the damn company won't.

He said this seriously, I noticed, though maybe with a kind of bullshit drama too. There was another Indian fellow eating lunch with us, and I looked over at him. And this one looked up from his lunch pail and grinned and said, That stuff he keeps in that little bag keeps him up too. And he pinched up his fingers to his mouth like it was a roll-your-own he was holding and sucked at it. And grinned and laughed. So I grinned too.

Well, they were young fellows. I got along with them. One of them talked about what the mining companies were doing to the land. That was the younger one. He'd go on about whites and America and destruction. Shit. Shit like that. Which I go along with sometimes in agreement, but other times I don't. I worked with them and knew they were no different from myself and other workers who have to make a living at that kind of work.

But this time, that afternoon, when I was hiding, sitting on a rock by the cliff edge, I wasn't expecting anything. Just sitting there, kind of thinking, blue sky way out there, the wind cutting through the trees, listening to the silence. And then along with the breathing there was a kind of clacking noise too, like shells rattling together.

I looked at what the two Indians were doing. They had taken their blankets off and rolled them up and laid them aside on a rock. And then they took some things out of a bundle that they had strapped across each of their backs. I didn't know whether to keep watching or what. I mean, it was private, see, and I could see they were looking around like they might be checking to see if someone might be watching. When the younger man turned his head towards me, I ducked my head below his line of sight. I thought about my watching, and later I looked again. I had never seen anything like that.

My wife and I, and the kids when they were home still, shop in Grants, and we see lots of Indians. Just shopping. Weekends, Christmas, other days. They'll be buying the usual things. Lots of

flour like folks who make their own bread, like folks in West
Virginia when I was a kid did and still do. Lots of kids usually,
sitting in the backs of trucks out in the parking lot, some of them
not looking too well. Once my wife said, Those Indians never say
much. But they did, kids laughing and hollering, and older ones
talking among themselves. Probably arguing once in a while too.
People see people only in a certain way sometimes, the way they
want to see them, that happens.

Here I was, watching the two Indian men, wondering what
they were up to and wondering too what I was up to. Hiding like I
said I was doing.

The older one had a bundle in his hand. Sticks and feathers
wrapped up in cornhusks, it looked like. They'd gone over by a
rock that was split in half. A huge rock, even the halves were big.
They were turned away from me, and I couldn't see their fronts.
They stood by that huge split rock for a long, long time. When the
direction of the wind shifted towards me, I could hear something.
It was a kind of singsong. Words, Indian words, I suppose, but
spoken in a rhythm. Praying, that's what I figured. The Indians
were praying by the big rock split in half. I couldn't stop myself
looking at them, and somehow I couldn't help but feel it was
somehow fateful I happened to be there.

I'd come up here just to be by myself. Because . . . well,
because I like the quiet and the thinking that I do and sort of
studying things. I guess it's praying of a sort, yeh. And then it
seemed like I was part of what the Indians were doing. Like they
wanted me to be even though they didn't know I was there. The
wind would change and drift the sound away and then bring it
back, and it felt like I was part of that prayer that was going on.
Something like that. It was an odd feeling, and then not odd too.

When I was a boy in West Virginia, I'd look over the countryside and see how it was overturned by coal mining, and I would think of how it must have looked before all that mining—and still did, or does in some places. And I'd see something that was there, the meaning of something. That's what I was thinking.

The Indians I saw and watched put those sticks and feathers down into the crack between the big rock halves, down in there somewhere—that was the meaning of something. Then the two of them stepped back, put their stuff together, and said something to each other. And then they left. I watched them leave down the mountain slope. And I just felt, in fact I could see myself, like I was still hiding with the quiet and the mountain and the praying that had been going on.

Pennstuwehniyaahtse

Quuti's Story

Q uuti told me this story, Santiago said to Cholly.
Santiago and his twelve-year-old grandson were walking home to the Pueblo from their sheep camp in the mountain canyon. I don't know how much of it is true, but there are true things in it. He told it to me years ago, and it is about a time long before that, perhaps in those years when I was a little boy.

Quuti was already no longer a child when he was taken by some white people who were teachers of the belief of the Mericano.

Quuti said, We had been told this would happen. My grandmother was in great fear of them. When they would come around, she would take us children to the hills and hide us until they left. But it was one day when we were not prepared that they came. A man and a woman in a buckboard, and a man on a horse.

They just simply took me. They carried a piece of paper on which was written something that would require me to go with them. My grandmother and my mother and father protested, but it was of no avail. The Mericano teachers said our leaders had agreed. It was written in the paper they had. So I went. My family and I cried. My mother packed me something to take along for me to eat, dried meat and bread, what little we had. My father gave me a cornmeal pouch, which he told me to hide from the Mericano. The white people put me in the buckboard and away we went.

That evening just before nightfall we camped. We headed

east, but I didn't know then where we were, although years later I did.

The Mericano built a fire and cooked something. I took my carrying sack and started to eat my food that was in it, but the woman grabbed it from me and threw it away. The coyotes probably ate it. I started to cry because I was afraid they meant to starve me. Such things had happened to our people in captivity. I knew that from stories told by elder people.

The woman pulled me out of the buckboard and sat me down on the ground, and she gave me a bowl with mushy stuff, hard bread, and meat. I started to eat then, as I was happy they weren't going to starve me, but the woman grabbed my hand and put a metal thing in my fingers and stuck it into the meat. She was talking to me in her language, but at that time I didn't understand a word of it.

The woman then showed me how to eat by using her metal thing to put food into her mouth. I tried, but I was clumsy at it and kept dropping the food and the metal thing. I thought it would take me all night to eat my supper. I learned I didn't have to eat my bread with the thing, which I learned later was called a fork. I guess I started learning then how the Mericano lived their lives.

It is much simpler and easier, of course, to eat with the fingers, but they preferred to make it difficult. It makes them feel better, maybe more intelligent, maybe more skillful to live such complicated lives.

Quuti said things like that about the Mericano, Santiago said. He said he learned so many unnecessary and pointless things at the place where he was taken to. But he went ahead and learned because it was required. I became a good Indian, he would say and laugh.

Let's stop for a while, Good Indian, Santiago said to Cholly. They sat to rest by the roadside on a large rock.

Where did they take him, Nana? Cholly wanted to know.

After camp that night, they went to a large town where he was put on the train with other Indian children. Some were just little babies, Quuti said. We were all sad as we looked out the windows at the land flying away from us. Traveling for days and nights, we finally stopped, and later, after I learned some Mericano words, I could name the place. Pennstuwehniyaahtse. It was a school there, and that was the place where we were to learn how it was to live like the Mericano.

They taught us, or tried to, and we tried also because we had no choice. If we didn't try, we didn't get anything to eat, or we got locked up, or we had to do extra work until our hands would bleed. Most of us learned how to speak in the Mericano language, although it was hard to say the strange words. And to write them.

We could not speak our own languages because that was not allowed and because there was no one else who spoke similarly. We were all peoples who were different from each other. But we found ways, and we even learned ways to talk with each other even if we would be punished when we got caught. Sometimes I would go to the barn and talk to the cows. The cows would just look at me, of course, but at least I could hear myself and I would not forget the sound of my own language. I surely must have told those cows a lot of stories.

Cholly and his grandfather walked the many miles toward the Pueblo. There was no sound except for their footsteps, the calls of the crows once in a while, and Quuti's story being told by Santiago.

I stayed at the school called Carlisle, Santiago said Quuti said. Three years. One day, because I was fifteen years old I decided that

I had had enough of the Mericano's teaching. I was already a man and I was still being treated as a child by the Mericano. I was concerned that my parents needed my help. And I was worried—I thought about this a lot—that I was becoming more like an Mericano than one of our own people.

So I told the person in charge of us what I was thinking and about my decision. He stared at me for a while, and then he said, William—that was my Mericano name—you are a good Indian boy, and you're becoming a fine blacksmith. It is a good trade. The United States of America needs skilled workers like you for we are going to be the greatest nation in the world. I knew that I was never going to go home if I kept staying in that Mericano place. So I decided that I would leave that very night.

I told this Chisheh friend from San Carlos I was leaving. He was younger than me and he cried, but he wished me a good journey. We packed some food for me and a few clothes, and before I left that night he taught me a song in his Chisheh language that meant this: Run, the wind speeds you. Walk, the trees hide you. Speak, the birds hear you. Sing, your voice comforts you. It was a song prayer his people sang in their fight against the Mericano soldiers.

So Quuti left Pennstuwehniyaahtse, Santiago said. It must have been late autumn when he did because he got caught in a snowstorm not too much later on.

Cholly noticed that the afternoon sun was nearing the western horizon. They had walked for miles, and Santiago had kept up the same walking rhythm, never seeming to strain, his arms and hands swinging, once in a while indicating points in Quuti's story.

I had walked for many days, Quuti said. A heavy snowstorm came suddenly, and I almost froze. Never had I seen anything like that. It felt like the wind was blowing me more steps backward than I took forward. Finally, I found a barn in which I took shelter. I had to pull ice from my hair. There were cows in that barn, and they kept me from freezing. I think it was two days and nights that I stayed. The snow was as deep and high as the door of the barn, and the wind was blowing very bitter cold. I was afraid of the cold, and I was afraid of getting caught and sent back to the Carlisle school in Pennstuwehniyaahtse.

I didn't know what I should do, but finally I decided I would find the people who owned the barn and cows and tell them the truth. I would tell them I was on my way back to my home and people in the west, and I hoped they would have compassion and not report me to the government authorities. I was also very hungry. After many days of walking, I had run out of food, and I had only the cows' milk for nourishment. And so I started to dig out of the barn.

I had managed to push the barn door open a little and had begun to dig through the snow for a while when I heard a sound. I listened and it sounded like someone was digging too. And it was.

Suddenly the snow fell open and there was a man standing in front of me who was so startled he dropped his shovel. And then he said something, but I didn't understand him. I thought the cold had frozen my ears and brain so I couldn't understand or that I had so quickly forgotten the Mericano language. But I soon figured out it wasn't the Mericano language he was speaking. It was another language.

Anyway, I understood from the man's gestures that he had been digging a tunnel through the snow so he could get to the barn to see after his cows. He was worried about them. When he came into the barn and saw his cows, he was so happy to see they were alright he started to kiss them and hug them and rub their hides to warm them up. And talk to them in this strange language. And I knew then he wasn't one of the Mericano, for I had never seen any of them act like this man.

He was smiling and laughing because he was so happy. And then he started to milk the cows, whose teats were so full they must have been hurting. So I helped him. After we finished milking the cows and fed them, he pulled me along to his house through the tunnel he had made in the snow. A wife and children were there, and they all set to work in making me feel at home. I was still half frozen, and I had on clothes that were worn and dirty.

The man put me into a tub of warm water with soap, and then I was fed. All this time they were talking to me, but I couldn't understand them. And when I said a few things in the Mericano language, they couldn't understand either. So I said some things in our Indian language too, and it was all the same, and we got along just fine. I was happy to be warm and not hungry and freezing anymore, and the people in that family were kind, friendly, and compassionate.

I tried to explain from where I had been coming and where I was going, but it didn't seem to make any impression at all. After several days as I got my strength back I wanted to leave, but I owed that family something for saving my life and so I stayed for a few more days to help them out with their farm. I think by then the woman and man understood where I was headed and why. They indicated they wanted to help, but it seemed to them to be so far away where I was going and it was winter and fearfully cold.

Those people, they got me to understand that they knew about long journeys and enormous difficulties. They asked me to stay until the winter was over. So I stayed with them until spring came. We never spoke any of the Mericano language, but I learned to speak their language a little, and they learned to speak a little of ours, especially the children, a boy and a girl whose hair was so yellow it shone like the sun.

I have never forgotten them and their name. Yoonson. They were a fine and caring family. Yoonson. When I got married and my first son was born, I called him that name. Yoonson. That journey was hard, but if it wasn't for those people I would never have made it home.

Cholly could see the smoke rising from the chimneys in the Pueblo, and he was glad for that. He was tired, but his grandfather Santiago still seemed to be walking strongly along. The wind was colder now and had started to pick up briskly, and the sun had dropped below the western mountain ridge.

So Quuti arrived home safely. It was a long journey. I believe Quuti's story is mostly true, Santiago said. And with a warm smile he added, Quuti was a fine and good man.

When they arrived home and were warming themselves by the kitchen stove, Santiago said to Cholly's mother, That son of yours is quite a walker. He nearly walked my poor old man's legs off. He would have made beloved Quuti a good companion on his walk home from Pennstuwehniyaahtse.

About the Author

Simon J. Ortiz is a poet, fiction writer, essayist, and storyteller. He is a native of Acoma Pueblo in New Mexico, where he grew up at Deetseyaamah, a rural village area in the Acoma Pueblo community. He is the father of three children—Raho, Rainy, and Sara—and is a grandfather. As a major Native writer, he insists on telling the story of his people's land, culture, and community, a story that has been marred by social, political, economic, and cultural conflicts with Euro-American society. Ortiz's insistence, however, is upon a story that stresses vision and hope by creative struggle and resistance against human and technological oppression. His previous works include *Speaking for the Generations, After and Before the Lightning, Woven Stone, Fightin', The People Shall Continue, Howbah Indians,* and others. He has received award recognition from the National Endowment for the Arts, the Lila Wallace–Reader's Digest Fund Award, a "Returning the Gift" Lifetime Achievement Award, and a New Mexico Humanities Council Humanitarian Award. Presently he lives in Tucson, Arizona.